Also by Jim

nc
GoodCopBadCop
Good Cop
the Light

graphic novels
Savant
Gabriel

Ava

Ta v. much!

for Ahm

Rerun to Eden

RERUN TO EDEN

Jim Alexander

Planet Jimbot
Glasgow

Rerun to Eden is copyright 2023 Jim Alexander.

The moral right of the author has been asserted.

All characters and events in this publication, other than those clearly in the public domain, are fictitious and any resemblance to real persons, living or dead, is purely coincidental.

All rights reserved.

No part of this book may be reproduced or transmitted in any form or by any electronic or mechanical means, including photocopying, recording or by any information and retrieval system, without the written permission of the author, except where permitted by law.

ISBN (print): 978-1-9164535-8-6
ISBN (digital): 978-1-9164535-9-3

Rerun to Eden is a legally deposited book at the National Library of Scotland, Edinburgh.

For LC

EDEN

It was morning and the world was still alive.

Was it light outside? Administrator Aran supposed it must be. He could not remember the last time he felt the rays of the sun on his face. Although he was sure there was a last time. And at the time, he was certain it would probably have seemed the most innocuous thing. Like a warm sheet; a comfort blanket; or transportation to another place. A memory of mother. A type of mother he could not possibly have had.

Not that he would have missed any of it. Why lament the untouchable? The insensate? The painfully emaciated wash of time across the border that separates what was real and what was falsehood? The pursuit of an electrical discharge that persists only in the organ that takes up space between the ears?

The reality, cold or hot, dependent on one's perspective, was that if Aran stood outside without the protective layers of his suit wrapped around him and took a walk, things would get complicated for him very quickly indeed. The environment wouldn't kill him straight away. There would come about pressure points in the nerves, in the veins, and these would build to the point they'd turn the body inside out. The pain would be excruciating and prolonged. He knew this in the way he didn't have to tip a pot of scalding hot water over him to know it would not be good for his complexion. Likewise, he didn't have to experience the rapacious blistering of his lungs to accept that not venturing outside was a complete no-brainer.

That is without the suit; a large clunky thing which hung in a capacious compartment in the equipment room, enshrouded in unbreakable glass, gathering dust for all he knew. Tensile neglect for all he cared.

He was a citizen content to be bereft (and safe) in an expanse of sterile, cracked wasteland. Not any kind of Badlands, but one embroidered by sensor-driven tracker weaponry. The occasional emergence and atomising of the odd desert rat only emphasising the overkill in play. Perhaps such a state of affairs was brought about at the behest of his predecessor? Or the predecessor of his predecessor? No matter, it was part of Administrator Aran's dowry. It was that and the hermetically sealed tower that stood over a click tall, which he called home.

No, not home. Such a notion did not sit well with Aran and his Administrator sensibilities. It had to be something else, then. Did it matter? Was it crucial? Details could be important. His surroundings could be important. Permanent residence would be a better description.

The clock was ticking. That was important, too.

He occupied the top level of the Tower mainly, known as the Hub. Ensconced in a big machine room, but close enough to the observation lounge for him to peer at the rolling vista outside. If he chose to; if this was not the furthest thing from his mind. His bruised, shrinking mind.

Presently he was on the floor, on his side. Bubbles of toxin careening against his blood. Neurochemicals. A self-poisoning. A lacing of acetone. His head fit to burst. His mouth impossibly dry. Nearby, like a segment of a discarded limb, an empty bottle of Jim Beam lay mirroring his position on the floor.

Around him, banks of processors decked the walls, or the segments of wall not taken up by drinks cabinet and wardrobe. Machinery in its most fluid form coalesced around him. It created a fluttering effect around shifting screens, like intelligent confetti.

There was movement. A stem appeared, extended, segmented; taking on an artificial life of its own. The stem reached out for him and secured itself to the port at the back of his neck. And slowly it extracted the poison, replacing it with electrolyte.

All this was something of a daily ritual. And he was no different in this respect, looking back, than the caveman intoxicated on the juice of berries. He was no different than any other member of the dwindling human race. In the grip of a collective downward spiral, medicated up to the eyeballs, howling at a fragmented moon.

Becalmed neurotransmitters.

And suddenly, Administrator Aran's head didn't feel that big anymore, having fallen back in line with the rest of his body. He sat up reinvigorated and refreshed. He reached down and straightened the sides of his tunic. The collar around his neck was no longer a chain. No longer a fallen halo.

The extractor had flushed out his insides but had done little for his furrowed brow. It had done nothing to ameliorate the creases in his forehead. He was dragged from the cover of darkness that was a hangover, yes, but there was still the stress. The incessant waves of anxiety remaining. The need for stewardship. The overriding imperative and weight on his shoulders that was duty. The importance of guiding the human race into the 22nd Century.

The tunic was too informal an attire, he decided. "Wardrobe, I think." His voice was one of control, and this was his exclusive domain; it penetrated the very bowels of the Hub.

Administrator Aran took the necessary steps forward. The wardrobe contours shimmered as it phased in and out. As facades go, he preferred a more vintage feel. A virtual varnish finish. There were a number of linked recesses scattered around the Hub in different rooms. Each amounted to an ethereal presence, a portal as such, all leading to the same shared space. Interconnected interiors. He reached inside, past the facade, where his fingers took a stroll, tiptoeing along the railing there, which contracted and expanded at will, with hangers attached. When his hand happened upon his preferred choice, it set off a neural tingle.

Such technology was unique to this station. A perk of working and living in the Tower.

"The right side of pink." He pulled out the dress suit

attached to the chrome hanger. *Hugo Boss.* He held it out in front of him to better take in the latest manifestation of his personal taste. "Of course, it is," he said, pleased with himself.

Everything had to be perfect, or at least his idea of perfect, so *of course* he picked that suit. It struck a note, resurrecting something long stayed with him. He was reminded of audio played to him back in the day as he reached maturation in the womb monastery. The story was a masterwork, a great example of American literature, describing a world long gone even before civilisation fell off a cliff.

There was a phrase back then, maybe he was paraphrasing, he was a baby after all, but the line stuck with him nonetheless. *The right side of pink.*

There were others like him, tasked to implement his decisions on the ground, but it was only Administrator Aran who occupied the Tower.

The reason for the change of attire was as old as civilisation itself. He was expecting company.

*

Outside, a copter approached.

Blocky, heavily armoured, nuclear powered. Its giant rotor blades chopping through the dense environment, asserting dominion, mastering the tyranny of the air. The blades created a series of wind tunnels, the force of which carved out tracklines on the topsoil below.

"A friendly," said the pilot on comms, having

already announced their impending arrival to Tower protocols.

Inside the copter were four occupants: one civilian, the rest military personnel. The captain sat impassively in a military chem-suit, consisting of non-reflective material and a breast-holstered gun. Infrared goggles hung listlessly from his neck. No sign of a gas mask. He was in debriefing mode.

"There are a select few," he said, "who wield complete control over countries and continents. There is no denying they run the world."

A mood shift registered on the captain's face. His natural instinct was to err on the succinct, but in light of the subject matter, such talk of titans, he granted himself a greater latitude. "Or what's left of the world."

His eyes, chiselled by the decades, fell on the Bequeathed sat across from him. "You are to be taken to one such man," he continued. "There is a directive that an Administrator's period of solitude does not extend beyond three years. You have been selected and screened. For seven days you are to be his companion."

Careful not to allow his gaze to linger. If looks could kill, or lead to court martial.

"That is all."

*

There was a noticeable change in pressure. The descent of metal into something malleable, enveloped by filtered air. At the end of the process, there was a breathable atmosphere. There was the application of boots on the ground.

The enclosed landing area now behind them, Bequeathed and armed entourage converged on the Tower Hub. Their ears collectively popped. Nanobots, externally facing, filled the ether, coating an extra protective layer of epidermis to their exposed skin.

Administrator Aran was there to greet them. He was joined by his sole companion, which floated at his shoulder. It was his *Familiar*, a bubble droid, rare enough these days to be considered almost antique. Should anyone pose a threat to its lord, master and protectee, it would facilitate the vacating of air from an intruder's lungs. And then dissect them into perfectly symmetrical pieces where they stood.

His sole companion up to this point: the party facing Administrator and Familiar were very much expected.

Aran raised his hand, which was sufficient to signal many things, but in this instance bring the soldiers to a halt. He turned the same hand 180 degrees and ushered the Bequeathed forward; appraising her all the while. She was tall and slender, imparting elegance in every sense of the word. Her clothing had an iridescent quality, enhancing the fluidity of her movement as she walked. She had dark skin. Darker than his. More beautiful than his.

She was calm personified. Aran had heard that the blood pressure of the Bequeathed never changed from 110/90, and he had no reason to doubt the veracity of this. Instantly, she looked like she belonged. A mental fog descended and Aran struggled to remember a time she was not a part of the Hub.

She would be provided with her own quarters for the duration of her stay. And her own wardrobe. There was no escaping the obligation.

"My name is Rhonda," she said.

"Aran," he said. "Administrator."

No further information or conversation was forthcoming. There was a trace of a central African accent in her voice, but Aran couldn't pinpoint the area exactly.

For a moment, the fact of this annoyed him.

Such was the substance of their first meeting, the prospect of a handshake had now passed. An embrace was out of the question.

He changed his attention to the group of soldiers, who continued to hang back. With a flick of the hand, they could consider themselves dismissed. Like Administrator Aran himself, he was certain they had more important jobs to do.

They stood in silence on the observation lounge, watching the copter make its departure. They peered on as the rotor blades ate up the vista, making it seem even more endless than would first appear. Aran was aware that he needed downtime, and this was it.

Both were statuesque, no noticeable fault lines. Except for a single glance from Rhonda towards the bubble droid, which maintained a discreet but viable distance from them. It would be remiss of the type of person Aran was not to notice.

"You have a question?" he prompted.

"Yes…no, I…" Her structured demeanour said nothing of an emergent tumult underneath.

"That's fine. Perfectly acceptable. Please, you are my guest."

"Is it AI?"

"My Familiar?" he said. "A very early form, not obsolete, not like the others, but yes, it fits the bill. It was left behind to guard over us. The Tower couldn't operate without it.

"A parting gift."

"Do you think they will return?"

Right then, they looked at each other, and it felt like they were meeting for the first time.

"I have faith," he said. "Unshakeable, enduring, immovable. I find that this is enough."

The conversation was over. Both turned towards the observation screen once more to refamiliarise themselves with the scorched earth. The copter, just visible in the horizon, was barely a speck in the sky. Blink and each of them would have missed it.

*

Having changed into a new suit, light blue—*Tom Ford*—Aran walked into the grand dining room. He sat at the circular dining table and looked up. He leaned back in his chair, staring at the chandeliers hanging above him, suspended from an impossibly smooth ceiling. The chandeliers were encrusted in jewels, which caught the artificial light, forming geometric shapes of several layers of complexity. Without fail, this had a soothing effect on him. It helped clear the mind.

He wasn't made to wait too long. Dressed in a crepe couture *Valentino San Gallo* dress, she glided in to join him, demonstrating the grace of movement of someone who could rise effortlessly above a state of flux. Hers was a life of being ushered from room to room, compartment to compartment; interconnected corridors.

Burundian. Aran finally had to swallow his pride and acquiesce a neural spike so revealing her full bio. Accessing her whole life before him in script. She was Burundian.

Before them, there were several small bowls and a platter of bread products. Riding the beams, succumbed to a gentle slingshot, which all done, saw the dishes trac'd from an adjoining kitchen and served at their table.

"We eat," he said. "Bread rolls and American stew."

Rhonda was lost in thought. Laid out in front of her was enough food to feed several families from her home village. And so, she ate, her training would not permit any other course of action. She found her surroundings strange and disconcerting, but this did not bemuse or unsettle her. She was detached. It didn't take the whole of her to play her part.

Aran was visibly restless: the straightening and bending of legs, shifting his weight from one side of his chair to the other. He scooped up a chunk of meat from a bowl and without ceremony plopped it in his mouth. But it proved too big and unwieldy a piece, no matter how ferociously he chewed.

He was unconcerned with breaking the silence. They had already talked, and now the moment had passed. In no mood to claw it back.

But there were still words. "Forgive me," he said, before thinking better of it, and before getting to his feet. "Excuse me," he said.

He left her to what remained of her meal.

A short time later and he was a different animal. Dressed in gym gear, he hit the exercise room. He ran on a treadmill, surrounded by a multitude of carefully choreographed holographic vignettes agitating for his attention.

He was annoyed with her. Deeply frustrated at the situation he found himself in. Not a peep out of her; she sat like a startled fox, a church mouse, with nothing in terms of conversation. And then the self-chastisement. Why should he concern himself with the likes of her? Why have her here in the first place? What could possibly be gained, over such a short time, from him not being alone and left to do the work?

His crashing feet on the moving surface kept in line with his heartbeat. Simple design; nothing too cluttered. He was flanked by images of various terrains, all barren. One of desert; another of rocks; another of a dead blackened forest; a fourth dominated by a half-buried skeleton of a cow. When he ran, he liked to be stimulated within and without. He liked to be reminded of the stakes.

There had been *The Collapse*. No one could be sure when the phenomenon first reared its head, revealed its initial tentative steps, possibly twenty, maybe even thirty years ago, but the fact was irrefutable that all life was dying. Living material becomes inert, having lost along the way the basic biology required to be able to reproduce. To reproduce itself. To reproduce anything. Animals did not die instantly but an expiry date was written in their DNA.

Humanity in conjunction with the AI community had tried to find a cure, but a wholly synthetic solution had so far eluded them. This prompted the AI to withdraw, fold into itself, lost in the tundra of cyberspace, vowing to return, but only if and when it had a cure. To find a solution where organic life could be brokered from non-life.

What evidence AI ever existed rested in Aran's care. There was his Familiar. There was the Tower. Aran could not hope to run the latter without the former.

There was only one Tower. The sole wonder of a diminished but new world. Its technological marvels could not exist outside a fixed point. Its primary purpose was at present unknown.

It could not be duplicated or broken down or packaged up and then despatched to other parts of the world. There was no prospect of using it to, for example, supply enough power to light up a city for a year. It was part of a grand design unknown even to it. It demonstrated the patience of a foot soldier. Playing sentry, waiting to escort its architects back to this world, should such an eventuality ever come to pass.

And humanity's role in all of this was so much less. Administrator Aran was raised to live in the Tower and use it for a purpose that served the interim. Humanity was never meant to understand its part in the Grand Design in order to fully accept it. And he was humanity. Nothing existed outside of him. Nothing else mattered. He took meticulous care; he worked out, drank, dressed, and breathed in clinically fresh air, doing the bidding of absentee gods.

And he ran, and the sensory saturation continued. Flanked by screens now showing animals long extinct. A dodo here, a Tasmanian tiger there.

Sweat ran down his face, a desired by-product of his current choice of activity. A lion on one screen, an elephant on the next. For Aran, it was the ones he remembered as a child that really hammered home. Of what was at stake. The consequence of failure.

It wasn't enough to just sit tight and wait for the AI cavalry to arrive. There was the belief, then the hope, that they would have to return at some point. But even the notion of waiting—of anything connected with the concept of time laid bare—was precarious in itself.

Should AI return victorious, like new gods on their cyber chariots, the trick was to ensure there'd be enough of the human race still around to greet them. To give thanks. To dance and rejoice. To be saved.

It was a constant reminder. A constant in a lifetime

of constants. With such thoughts blazing a trail through his skull, the treadmill came to a stop, and so latterly did he.

*

She came to his bed in the middle of the night. She climbed on top of him. Seamless. He was ready to meet her. And in return, her kisses were perfunctory. She was there; she was not there. An absence of soul, and her mind was not required. Nor was his. They were each other's reflections.

Outside, the dusk winds rose. Incessant and unbowed, strong enough to strip the meat from your bones.

A memory. She was back in the copter, reaching up, taking grip of the strapping, accepting the offer of rigidity. Suddenly, inexplicably, a shift in the axis. There was a burning sensation in her head. She was seized by a notion, alarmed at the prospect of falling from the sky, her exposed body catching fire in the non-red sun. Fully ablaze before she hit the ground. Now, she would take this memory, this sensation, which some, her mother superiors included, may identify as evidence of weakness, and turn it on its head. She'd use it to drive her on. Embrace the inevitable.

The bubble droid floated near the open doorway. Filters up, it took the form of a shimmer, barely perceptible, a ripple in the air the only evidence it was ever there. A voyeur. A companion. A bodyguard.

One that can distinguish the grunting and thrusting played out in front of it as something other than an assassination attempt.

Diligently, they went through the motions. Turning. Two sets of skin that stubbornly remained cool to the touch. Eventually, he succumbed.

Administrator Aran shut his eyes and meditated on the rivulets that coursed inside of him, ushering the tension out of his arms and legs. When he opened his eyes again, she was gone, like she was something of a ghost.

There was no trace. There was no heat.

He got out of bed. There was a dressing gown draped over the bottom of the bed. He put it on. Minutes later, for want of a less crude measurement of time, he had a glass of whisky in his hands.

In no time, he was back in the Hub proper. The machinery and walls seemed more familiar to him, now the sweat had a chance to grow stale on his skin. Standing there, as way of an afterthought, he realised his hand was on his chin. Now he'd brought it to his attention, he saw no reason to take it away. There was a strange taste in his mouth. An earthy taste. Dry. Everything about him was dry.

Surrounding him, shifting and adjusting to his movement, was a holographic map of the mainland. It served as a vivid reminder. It represented his latest mission. The world was in crisis and he was tasked with coming up, however temporarily, with a fix. Piece by piece, tipping point by tipping point, continent by continent. It wasn't purely ego to state that

Administrator Aran represented a last and only hope. The knowledge followed him around. Sticking plaster by sticking plaster. He wore it like a cloak.

With an upward thrust of his hands, he flexed the image forward, a flourish, orchestrating with his arms, causing it to unfurl like a sheet, flattening and opening out in front of him. The map's colour scheme was predominantly rust brown, of broken savannas and expanding desert. It was an arrangement that did not respect borders. In contrast, he could just make out impoverished patches of blue and green dotted across the landmass, imbuing the most meagre of returns. No matter how much he tried to formulate a recovery plan, no discernible pattern made itself known to him. For the life of him, he could not connect the dots.

He was no knight in shining armour, not yet. No closer to a solution. *She* was a puzzle he could not work out. *He* was a puzzle he could not work out. *Africa* was a puzzle he could not work out. The human race was a broken toy. One that the toymaker could not repair. But still, somehow, they had to find a way to keep going. For some of them, at least, to keep living.

He stood screaming. It was a silent scream, but his throat was raw and hurt like hell all the same. No prospect of the taste ever going away.

There was no release. No end in sight, except in the threat of failure.

His gaze fell on one of the dots, central, nudging towards the east. Nothing large or spacious. Nothing particularly strategic, but it had a name. Names could be important in their own way. Landlocked, situated in the Great Rift Alley, south of the Equator. It was Burundi.

*

They met again the following evening. He had spent most of the day in meditation. Having explored the permitted levels, she'd come across a maze at the far side of the Tower. When she reached its centre, she lay down in a pool of crystals where a memory of childhood became vivid and whole in her mind. As a child, she would often imagine herself as a four-legged creature running through the fields as fast as her legs could muster. And so, it came to her.

This time round, they found each other in better humour. It was time to eat.

They sat down to dishes of Marahagwe, Ugali and Boko Boko Harees. The colours, heat and scents of the food assailed the senses. They represented the closest thing to truth to emerge between them so far.

"Please forgive my manners from before," he said, nearly saying *you caught me at a bad time* but stopping himself short. Constantly thinking. Then, thinking better of it.

He stretched over to take her hand. She of course acquiesced, playing her part. He could comment as matter of fact on his own behaviour. She could not.

He kissed her hand. "Excuse me," he said. "Enchanté, I've not been quite myself."

She surveyed the several dishes in front of them, the blends, the aromas, and found none of it inauthentic. "This could be a family meal," she said, "in better times."

Aran fought the compulsion to shift in his chair. "You would have gathered all together, yes? As a family unit? The idea of several people together in the same place? Just to eat? How many must there have been of you? Four, five?"

"Oh, fourteen, fifteen of us," she said. "At least."

They stared at each other. His eyes widened and hers narrowed. Momentarily, their masks, the default glacial expressions, the overly-rehearsed mannerisms, had slipped. They viewed each other as below themselves, below what it was in their estimation to be human. To have and to make a point, and to have something to aspire to. They saw each other as barbarous.

"Who's counting?" he said, finally.

Everything was reduced to family trees and units. Humanity was broken but there was no easy fix. Such a thing could only come at a cost. An impossible cost. A terrible cost.

Still, getting her to think of her family relaxed her. And by way of osmosis this relaxed him.

"Do you think they'll come back?" she said. "Do you think there will be a cure?"

He was aware of everything in the room. Acutely so, as if extensions of him. The chandelier hanging from the ceiling. The length of her hair. The direction it flowed, the space it occupied. The feel of both chair and dining table. The cotton napkins and silver cutlery on display. The breaking of bread.

The foundation—the holy house—she belonged to would have swooped in like a bird of prey and plucked her from her family as a child. They would have shaped her, trained her, meticulously dismantling her, before piece-by-piece rebuilding, the culmination the object of perfection that presently sat in front of him. She was as much a product of constructed reality as he was.

"Please eat," he said.

*

A pattern was set. She appeared to him enshrouded in darkness. He in turn reached out and embraced a shadow. It would prove a diversion. No closer to completing his assignment.

After they made love, she lay on her side, her expression unreadable, and unpalatable. He took this as a sign she had already left. However, the truth of the matter was more mundane. It didn't make any material difference to her should he go or stay.

The Hub was calling to him, but even if this wasn't the case, he would have ended up there anywhere.

"Bourbon," he said.

Her being in the shadows made him feel like he was in the shadows. He didn't want to acknowledge the presence of his Familiar, but all there was, even if he looked hard enough, was a shimmer, a kinetic stream, a change in density. A glass of Woodford Reserve

Double Oaked appeared in his hand. Like magic. One he'd long accepted as truth.

This was the modern age, a time of reflection. And so he reflected. Where the underpinnings of the bible, of human tolerance and understanding, were rewritten. The revision of the sanctity of life. And he was a student of the new scripture; learned it by rote in part to secure his present vocation.

There was a sizzle, a slight charge in the air. He drank his drink and tried to empty his head, which was brimming with bullet point instructions. If only inspiration came with alcohol, he protested, or good living, or the snap of a finger.

*

The days that followed took care of themselves. Her time was taken up by ennui, memory and perfunctory acts. She accepted all of it.

The bubble droid was in attendance as ever, barely seen and never heard. Only when its logarithms dictated so. It demonstrated all the attributes of a floating lifeguard, serving to exist simultaneously between Administrator and Bequeathed, even when occupying opposite sides of the Tower. Never to be lost in its presence. Wrapped up in their trajectory as much as they in its. Drifting through corridors, through rooms, through thoughts.

After the first evening, Administrator Aran disowned the pink suit. He subsequently moved through the blues—Frost blue, Powder blue, Florentine,

Verdigris, Celestial blue—while she wore yellows, greens and grey. There was little in this to heighten the mood or alleviate the tension. Their colours did not gel. Shading to see out the coming storm. Strangers to each other.

It was time to eat again, but this time she barely touched the food in her bowl. Her head angled upward in a way that didn't quite say defiance but could accommodate a glint of nostalgia, a smattering of conviction. It was there in her eyes.

"My village…" she said, before fading off, afraid her words may conspire against her. Trip her up.

"Pardon?" he said.

She breathed in the purified air all around. It filtrated through her. It pushed her on. She was falling through the sky, slowly catching fire. "In Burundi, I left when I was six years old, but despite all the memories of civil war, the arid soil, the eternal drought, my village found ways to never prosper, but to continue nonetheless."

She could not look at him, but her words were meant for him. There was no one else. "You have great power. You are a powerful man. You can change things. Certain people, certain places. You can turn things around. You can draw a line."

She looked around, her head circling as if following a buzzing insect. "You live alone in so much space and have everything that any man could ever want or need…"

"…Except heart," she said.

He listened to what she had to say. He placed his

fork slowly down on the table, demonstrating suffi-cient care which suggested a measure of control, a more impulsive action buried inside of him. One, if released, would be enough to bring the Tower crash-ing down around their ears. The tension crept like a centipede across his shoulders. His eyes were incred-ibly dry. For a second, he could have sworn she was no longer in the room.

Later, they had sex, rarely straying from a single position. He used the curvature of her shape as a guide, wrapping himself in her skin.

"Do you think they will return?"

That wasn't the right question. The correct one would have been, *"Do you think we can survive?*

"Long enough?

"To see it happen?"

The imperative to prolong existence in some form. To make a commitment, written in blood, sweat and tears. There was faith out there among Administrator circles; a need to hang on until the turn of the 22nd Century. If you repeated the mantra long enough, then on some level you might believe it to possess a kernel of truth. That somehow getting over the line, getting to the next century, was elixir in itself.

There were still some thirty years to go. Adminis-trator Aran had as good a chance as any of seeing it through. He was something of a chosen one. But what of everyone else?

He clicked his finger and at the tail of a shimmer, like a pot of gold at the end of a rainbow, there was another drink in his hand. The last couple of days he had hardly eaten. He couldn't put it all down to stress, the dread of falling debris, the feeling of attending his own crucifixion.

A tunnel appeared in front of him, but it was a trick of the light, and once his eyesight adjusted, it proved to be a map of Africa all along. He drained the liquid. He allowed himself a moment of satisfaction as he studied the empty glass he now held up to his face.

"Yep," he said.

"You have everything that any man could ever want or need..."

The map was fully holo-programmable, touch-sensitive. It would collect mental stimuli and record his thoughts at the time of contact. As he paced across the room, it followed like a faithful hound, forming a circle around him. A sheet. A blanket.

He stood in awe.

Each segment matched the boundaries of various countries—or groups of smaller countries—that make up the continent. Here was the *mother of mankind*, the *Garden of Eden*. Humanity took its first tentative steps here. It was Aran's sworn mission that such a state of affairs should continue.

Previously he'd tried to link the countries that still had resources, however negligible. Logistics would not support this. He'd tried, he'd failed. Never anything other than a non-starter.

His digital focus fell on the zigzag segments of Central African countries. The thing to be done, finally, was to pick an area and be done with it. He stretched out; he decided. An index finger touched the appropriate pixels, the tip of the finger pulsating, the distal phalanx erupting into life, exposing a point in current time. A diagonal fault line appeared before him. It represented one last chance.

"*To never prosper, but to continue nonetheless.*"

It was settled, then. Everything above the line would be discarded, everything below to make the most of what little way of resource was available. And where to draw the line?

*

It was the seventh day, and another *thwip-thwip* pitted the sky. An approximation at least. A signature of sentience. This was noted and reported within the confines of the Tower, and like moving figurines having emerged from a cuckoo clock, Administrator Aran and Bequeathed Rhonda stepped out once more.

They were in the departure lounge. They could hear the approach, the crunching echo of soldiers' boots. The nanobots, where instructed, could have muffled the sound or erased it entirely, but Aran preferred it this way. Despite appearances to the contrary, he wasn't a fan of silence. Not always. Anything to displace the background noise going on inside his head.

And anyway, in a small way, however pitiful, here was evidence of life.

Rhonda kept her head bowed, careful to limit movement, her thoughts already confined to stasis.

She could have sworn drifting through the air was the odour of oily discharge, but such a thing, in such an environment, was impossible. She sensed a set of eyes on her, but when she looked up all she could see was the Bubble Droid several feet away bobbing in the ether.

The soldiers marched into view. None of the personnel, dressed in chem-suits with rifles strapped over their shoulders, were recognisable from the previous landing party, but this was as it should be. They were strangers on arrival; they would remain strangers when they departed.

Aran wore a tunic-styled top. Rhonda was back in civilian camouflaged apparel.

"Thank you," he said.

To whom the words were directed, she had no idea. It left her unconcerned. She was sure of the fact that, over the last seven days, she had performed every duty expected of her. The expression of thanks was neither expected nor coveted. It was not in her remit to desire anything for herself. This was not her purpose.

The soldiers continued to advance and she took some steps forward herself to join them.

The Administrator's gaze followed her. She could feel the intensity clip the back of her skull. She toyed with the idea of looking back. But there was too little distance still between them. The thought that something was still expected of her.

They were stone pillars. Cavernous landslides of emptiness, and it felt like they had both turned full circle. And then something moved. For a moment, a second one, their masks were askew; not sitting quite right on their faces.

She turned, gliding on her heels, and noted immediately there was a look of wistful fondness about him as he in turn studied her face. In return, she smiled a tight nervous little smile. There was some light in her eyes.

There was a soldier on either side of her, ready to escort her off the Hub. In a few short moments, it would be like she was never there. All they had to do was wait.

He could have said his goodbyes. He could have let her take her leave with at least something. Something human, something worthwhile, something benign. A glimmer of hope. If he had come to know anything about her, right there and then, slowly fading from view, she would be thinking of her village. Her childhood home. She would be thinking of Burundi.

Instead, his face darkened, was hard and unflinching, and instantly she knew what this would mean. It served to extinguish the light.

"I drew a line," he said.

She twisted round, bolted for him. Time stood still around them. There was only her and him. And she was upon him. She pounded her fists on his chest.

"Mercy," she said.

And he could afford her mercy for her present insubordination. The mercy he could not show her village. She would be returned to her foundation. She was chosen in her youth, at the point of the flowering of her natural beauty. Her family could not resist. The fates were already written. Cascading providence. Interconnecting corridors.

Her reality was that she would never return to her village. She would never hear from her family. It should make no material difference to her. Ignorance would be her shield. The absence of thought and memory.

A line was drawn by Administrator Aran. Those on the wrong side of the line would not be allowed to suffer. An induced type of sleep would be prescribed. A form of permanence. It was those on the *right* side who would shoulder the expectation of eking out some kind of existence, which could be best described as no life at all. Her village was on the wrong side.

Her village was on the right side.

She looked into his eyes with a surprising fierceness. She knew what he was capable of. Before now, she had failed to recognise it. Perhaps she had underestimated him. And now it was too late for even that. Too late to offer, or be in receipt of, even the feeblest of explanations.

The soldiers caught up with her and dragged her away, acutely aware that they were handling something luxurious and rare, but they had a job to do nonetheless. She would not struggle; she would not force the emotions back down. She'd lock them away.

One of the soldiers with minimum movement placed a gas mask over her face for safety. For hers and theirs.

All Administrator Aran could do was stand deathly still and, this time, watch her go. There was no mercy to be had. Not in this world. Still, he could not help but compliment himself on the bravery he'd shown in the moment. It would have been easier just to look away.

Finally, he reflected, between them, there was some heat.

*

Thwip-thwip.

The noise of the departing copter's rotor blades was trapped inside his head. As an accompaniment, the sensation of ridged glass was pressed against his lips. Vapours of saffron, liquor and allspice spread through the buccal cavity. Diving headfirst into moderately cold waters. Big splash.

Later that night, he both slept and dreamed alone. It was a dream of walls and suggestion. He couldn't get a grip on it. The soles of his feet on a slipping sliding surface. Shutting his eyes, despite knowing there was a chance he would never open them again. He would no longer have a use for them. Alone in his Tower, he was the sole representation of human ingenuity, the closest a human could be to godhood.

The Tower comms remained open, making sense of the static, waiting impatiently for an answer, which had become something else entirely.

He was falling. From the corner of his eye, he saw that his Familiar was falling too. He fell into a Faraday

Cage, which didn't appear to be rooted to any ground. A metal grid casing formed symbols within symbols that were unfamiliar to him. They were part of, at least up to now, an undiscovered language of the universe. The sky around him and the cage were dark, and seemed to get darker still. There was a change in pressure, a cracking of the air, as if something unfeasibly large, too great in scale for the unenhanced human eye to even fathom, was starting to move. He spied the droid outside, his faithful Familiar circling the cage. Sometimes, truth could only be visible from the corner of your eye. Sometimes when you looked straight at something it would be invisible. It was space. It was darkness. *I need to get out now,* he told it. But the droid continued to float and eddy like it belonged in the continuous darkness. For there was no escaping this. There was nowhere else to go. A rolling black cumulus spanned the horizon. Storm clouds had gathered.

The closest a human could be to godhood. But not quite. AI would descend eventually in the form of raindrops, passing through structure, absorbed by the skin. Weaving into his DNA and eventually replacing it.

*

He'd fallen asleep in his bed but woke on the floor next to a pile of empty bottles. He got up sluggishly, carefully, creating distance between him and the moving floor. Diverting a hand to his head, a futile attempt to short-circuit the pounding. The drinks cabinet, having reached its predetermined daily limit, was laid bare. And so was he.

He was too important an individual to feel this way. To be in such a stupor. It shouldn't compute. Unshaven. Dishevelled. Terrifying, stultifying…

Too hot, head fit to burst. And now he was locked in, frozen, and about to vomit and faint. He was outside, while inside, and the world without, within, was killing him. About to explode, implode, as if time wasn't pressing enough. As if it didn't matter at all. She was no longer in the picture. The remnants of something slicing through air.

There was the Hub. The soft thrum and throb of wall-to-wall machinery. Emerging from the apertures, various malleable, semi-transparent tendrils snaked towards him. A hypodermic needle attached to the end of every stem.

There followed a series of punctures along one side of his neck, the top of one of his arms. Instantaneously, his eyes closed tight as the rejuvenating effects took hold. A dark liquid running through him.

And in the background, enveloped in a gaseous shroud, was the bubble droid. His Familiar. A sphere. A silent sentry protecting him from the depths of himself.

It was the next day and the world was still alive. His next mission came into focus, and through this, came into being. A colour scheme featuring all shades of grey. A landmass resembling an arm gently crooked at the elbow. The scale of it. The magnitude.

He needed to be sober. He had his latest assignment. He needed to be steady and well. He needed to click his fingers without recourse to recoiling at the sound. Time to think. Find room to breathe. A holographic map unravelled before him. His latest deadline already looming.

It was California.

MEAT SPACE

Back on the slab and it was cold. Experiencing cold for the first time in a long time. I shivered.

Even so, my senses were overheating, overreaching, but the main emotion I was feeling was disgust. Such was the harshness of my current reality. The diktat handed to me by my present situation. I was faced with having to swap identity fluidity for brand loyalty. To exchange the ability to ride on my thoughts—dive and soar, soar and dive—for the restraints of a distressingly physical body. The need to defecate, and the desire to fornicate—I mean who, pardon my French, the *putain* wanted to *baise-moi* anymore?

I was emasculated. I was emaciated. Skinny and raw. I was back in Meat Space.

Micro-pixelation turned to plastic cotton fibre, weaving, contouring, and I was wearing clothes again. A black faux-leather coat hung from one of my shoulders. In Meat Space you need to make an exhibit of yourself; embrace something that hailed from a darker, more organic time. I mean, what better representation than a reminder that we used to skin our bovine bro-sisters? I'm not shitting you. I mean, what an utterly miserable excuse for a sentient species!

Such bad thoughts and potty language. Oh, the profanity. The courser my choice of words, the more befitting it was in conjunction with the gutters which flowed beneath my feet. But, as well as look it, if I didn't speak the part, the indigenous population would sniff me out. They'd cut me up. Slice and dice me into cubes. I'd be ground down. Fed to the hungry worms.

Only moments before, I fell. The displacement existing between two disparate such places, one from the other, was notoriously hard to predict. You just hoped you weren't too far above ground level as you entered the last part of your trip. You might begin the journey on sure footing and end tumbling through the dimensions.

My descent was measured in quick-fast cuts. I experienced a period of discombobulation. I made contact with concrete, rolled, and fell down a hole in the ground. My physiology had to adjust and start turning with the world around me. I felt all there was to feel as I transitioned from a place of near-infinitesimal dimensions to one consisting of a dismal three.

It was a shallow hole. Even so, I made heavy work of it as I climbed out. Accompanying my scrambling motions, inside my mouth, I pushed my tongue down from upper to lower teeth and noted a layer of plaque was already formed there.

I stood in a backstreet. Hot steam rose up from vents on the sidewalk. Again, I had to adjust. It was a strange sensation feeling gravity exert its imprint on my spine again. It had been a year since I was last here. Or was it years? Years since I made the decision to pass over? Or maybe it was just a year?

I could have refused to go back, of course. But no one refused; no one that I could think of. I was selected by lottery, a fundamental machination of the Universe. Under such circumstances, a sense of obligation outstripped almost anything else.

My Bluetooth brain was rattling. There was something watching me. A Big One. Porous skin. A breathless, sagging sack of rattlesnakes. But despite the slovenly appearance, there was no relaxing around it. It had stings.

Every digit, every detachable limb, carried a hidden artery-slashing blade.

"Where-yah-at?" it asked.

"Marshlands," I said.

"Don't-smell-a-Marshlands," it said. "Don't-like-the-gib-of-yar-stink."

I bristled. Such an act came naturally, which was proof I was well on the way to fully acclimatising to this alien environment I found so unnervingly familiar. The truth was I hailed from the inter-dimensional AR known as *Godspace*, but I could not tell it that.

"A day and a half out of the marsh," I said, "how the nip and tuck you know how I smell?"

"Where-yar-tatts?   Won't-survive-with-no-tatts. Why-yah-in-city?"

It was a good observation, I had to admit. A pertinent question. The human race was shrinking and so was the world around it. Only one city left standing on this side of a punctured biosphere. And this was it, the here and now. Why would any Godspace-forsaken dope come to a battery dump like this?

"I…" I said. My voice was crisp and unequivocal as I pointed at my chest. "I wanna buy a new pair of arms."

It was meat and therefore prone to psychic suggestion. Demonstrating its servitude to key phrases, it reacted by smacking its hands together. *Wanna buy…* Amplified by my holographic outer skin, which harnessed acoustic transformation, I followed the vibrations of the clap which flew over my head, travelled some and set up a flare on its perimeter, perched over a location a click away. If you looked at it a certain way, a strategized twitch of the head, it could almost be the shape of an arrow on high in the sky. It was pointing downwards.

New arms…

I shifted my gaze from the arrow in the sky. There was the sound of retching at my feet. Big One was having a seizure, down on the floor, writhing, incoherent. I went to its aid, placing it in the recovery position, checking it hadn't swallowed its tongue. As I did so, ever conscious of its many blades, some fully drawn already, I was careful not to cut myself on its body.

Upon completion, unfazed, unhurt, using legs for the purpose they were originally designed for, I headed in the direction of the arrow. I walked among atrophied tower blocks. Buildings that had grown and died, now little more than outlines. Three-dimensional shadows. Anyone living above ground level faced a precarious existence, but it was not unheard of.

My legs were leaden. Every step taking me further

from home. It wasn't enough to be useful, taking in what was left of the world and polluting the senses. I knew somewhere in the urban murkiness surrounding me, angels lurked in the corners. At the very least to remind me why I was here. At the very most to spur me on.

I reached the point, rearing up at me, the front of the mall.

A walk through the mall, using this new body of mine, you could make a day of it. I didn't need any re-emergent memory to inform me of such. But more to the point, the arrow was gone now, having dissipated in the icy breeze, lost to the enemy of time, which was time again. However, its position was still fixed in my mind. It had its hooks in me.

It had pointed over the mall.

You could *really* make a day of it.

In Meat Space.

Always the doubter. Even though to the eye naked and altered they appeared fully functional, plonking one piece of timber tremulously in front of the other, I still wasn't convinced by the efficacy of my legs. But I was on a mission. This tiny world just got tinier as I shuffled through the sliding doors.

By contrast, and my mind couldn't help but dwell on this, the world that existed outside this world was boundless. A world of escape, where AI had abandoned itself to a fashion of cyberspace, fluid space, true reality.

Godspace.

It was an open invitation. Humans could enter

Godspace at any time. In return for a seat in paradise, all you had to agree to was a dissolution of the physical; the elevation of the spiritual. A painless decomposition. That, and participation in the occasional lottery. A lottery, on this occasion, which just so happened to give me back a body and send me here.

Inside the mall, there were blocks next to blocks, blocks inside blocks. A series of straight lines and ninety-degree corners. No hint of curvature.

The flicks were on my right-hand side, screening motion pictures based on various eviscerations of the human body. Such was the most popular film genre of the time. There was a rating system in place, dependent on whether someone with a degree of medical training was present during filming. Also, dependent on whether some form of anaesthetic was brought into play. The application of both sharp and blunt objects. The dominant quasi-religion at present was the Cult of Self-Worship and it was a fundamental requirement of its teachings to be familiar with the workings of the human insides, in all their lumpen glossiness. Currently showing, three to pick from, the motion picture experiences in no particular order: *Vivisection of the Damned*, *Enter the Interior: We're All the Same,* and *Sacks of Blood 4.*

It would be a game changer if Grunge took hold. Every movie, no matter how gruesome its contents, would enjoy a Universal rating.

My internal compass grabbed at me and instructed me to climb, so I took the binary escalator, which started as a single step then unfolded before me.

Binary in the sense it moved up and down dependent on what direction you wanted to go. Determining the direction was intuitive, and in so doing you needed, however temporarily, to open your thoughts. There was little point fighting it. I thought *up* and there I ascended.

As fate would have it, a figure sprung into view. It was enhanced with a buzzsaw for an arm; from my vantage point I couldn't make out the join. What I could be certain of was that it was heading my way. It was going down.

Angry Buzzsaw. As good a name as any. Draped in leather that sweated shit brown condensation. Assaulting every one of my senses, which screamed at the top of tattooed lungs *NONE-A-YER- BUSINESS.*

Maybe we could have passed each other, going our own particular way, whistling in the recycled wind, without incident. We would barely acknowledge each other, subservient as we were to a nascent conveyor belt of straps and transmutable metal. He was going up, I was going down, and we reached the point we were level with each other. It shouldn't have been, but it was. It was an eerie feeling.

An unfortunate by-product of thought-triggered mecha was the prospect of an escaping thought or two. Floating in the ether. Maybe the seeds of something that would ultimately give someone like me away.

As for it, it was screaming. Its thoughts gnarled and twisted, on the lines of: *MORON-IMBECILE-GUTS-FER-BRAINS!*

Words booming inside my skull, threatening to throw me off balance and blow a hole in my noddle.

For Angry Buzzsaw, a tsunami of thought processes, I shouldn't have made an impression. So much clutter and noise. With any luck the hullabaloo would drown out anything that could escape from my relatively restrained mind. The odd languid thought on the lines of: *The stretching of a wing to an nth degree, it occupies every point in time.*

Swallow and you would miss it, a so-so shifting in the density of the air. But after much stress and worry on my part, he was passing me, continuing to go down. I continued up, but even so, I took a moment to feel below the waistline to confirm the limbs down there were still part of me.

The noise was receding and I bit my bottom lip all the more to resist the temptation to look back. Then it got a whole lot louder!

MUTANT-BONBONS-MUTANT-BONBONS-MUTANT-BONBONS!

There was a pull. A bomb set off, occupying the space between us. There was the flare of screaming metal, slicing and adding to the buzz.

It was coming for me. Its section of the escalator moving up. Making up the space between us by taking every second step.

I braced.

OPEN-WOUND!

Lost-child.

TASTE-A-CATSHIT!

A nodule at the back of my head returned a Threat

Level of two. That low? Level two was a smidgen higher than the danger posed by walking on uneven concrete, or breathing in air. Something as paltry as this, though, meant I was on my own. Left to my wits. My own steam.

I turned to meet it. One swing. I was already off my feet. My legs, the source of so much recent consternation, proved my saviour, jumping several feet in the air. The buzzsaw sliced through the ventilated gas that occupied the gap. It came down. The stairs moved away, blade ending up embedded in the tracks. The escalator came to a jarring stop. Our thoughts once more exclusively our own. Angry Buzzsaw was bent over, trying to prise its appendage clear with its free arm. I was on a downward motion myself, but I was more mobile. No time like the present. Punching its face. Hard. There was a crack, we both heard it, as I dislocated its jaw.

It was a satisfying sound. My offending knuckle flaked broken skin, but otherwise, there was little discomfort. A little puffiness but holding firm. I revelled in it, the whole sordid business, but why would I find it so agreeable? Why so easy to transition from a wisp to a champion of chaos and frenzy, unless I was already assimilated? I was at one with the environmental grime around me. When I was reissued, they moulded me in a way that wasn't designed to fail.

As for Angry Buzzsaw, it was no longer interested in me. It was vulnerable and exposed, and its jaw needed fixing. At the very least, wired up. Maybe it would get a new one. One made from various metals.

And a new coat to go with it, exuding a different colour of sweat.

GOT-ME-FREDDY-FRANCES-GOT-ME-
I-GOT-GOT...

Buzzsaw, dislodged chin in hand, thoughts still screaming, just not wholly directed at me. Instead, the escalator swept it back up into the belly of the mall before taking a sharp corner and ushering it out of sight. I headed in the same direction, ascending, rolling, roiling, but all done at a more leisurely pace.

I reached the top of the escalator and was met by an expanse of white space, which peddled the illusion of pushing out boundaries. I stepped off and there was nothing much to do but continue on, taking a stroll past shops of lurid colours and guises. Stores that sold parasites and drums and the offer of all types of cosmetic surgery.

The latest craze was in skin removal. The exposing of ligaments and tendons, held translucent against the luminescence, was all the rage. Welcome to Meat Space.

There were other shoppers, twisting and gliding on a smooth surface, passing by, unable or unwilling to lift their patchwork heads, but moving slowly, careful not to bump into each other.

No one in the mall would meet my gaze. I realised then; I was bathing in rays of light. I looked up and saw a cloud of pale grey. Spongy, soft. Benign smoke obscuring the ceiling. In a strange way, it reminded me of Godspace.

All I wanted to do was soar. Immerse myself in the

expanse I had left behind. You see, I had already tired of the lump of meat I currently called a body.

There was a swirl of voices, an elemental chorus. but when I looked around, nobody's lips were moving. Enough people had to speak and whisper it conspiratorially for it to reach critical mass and hang in the air, so it was impossible for me to avoid it. I was a lightning rod to conjecture, another by-product of transition, I surmised. There was a rumour doing the rounds, with no accompanying answer, that lurking on the other side of the clouds were Peacekeepers: droids of imperious power and otherworldly density, ready to break through and keep the peace. Stop an ugly world from becoming uglier. The only criteria being that the human race—that rump, that naked sore that was left behind—would have to wish it so.

I wished it. Bound in aching singularity. I wanted so much to be swept away. That the droids would descend, making my need to be here redundant. But here I was, hollow, expecting no reward for my time in Meat Space. AI dealt in the long view. A viewpoint that could stretch into next to forever. It dealt in those types of algorithms.

It didn't matter how long the human race lasted. Time was not a concept AI held in any kind of esteem.

It was close. So tantalisingly close. A matter of footsteps, a matter of flight. An inch outside the periphery of your vision. A piece of meat could change everything about itself, just by choosing to pass through. Pass into Cyberspace. Dull solidity on one hand and blessed liquidity on the other. Even so, the reverse, which would see Godspace intrude on Meat Space, could never happen. Could never be true. Reality had its walls, and here I was, my body kicking in, juices sluicing around fatty white blood cells, having reached the point of no illusion. One-way traffic. I knew where I was and where I wasn't. But still, I wished it otherwise.

A dark cloud shifted and broke away from heaven. Almost tumbling, it floated down towards me.

It joined me as I stood outside the entrance to a flesh store. The arrow was gone but I could still feel its presence pointing down, oppressive, a slice of life, carving out the top of my skull and poking around inside. I knew this was where I was meant to be, in close proximity to a black cloud, which symbolically at least summed up my lot. My current existence in this current plane.

I walked through the door. A little bell sounded as it swung open. The bell set off a synaptic message, lighting up inside my cranium, rendering the message:

Make the aches and pains of bodily enhancement go away. Miracle Grunge keeping it flesh, fresh and spesh!

There were concurrent moving images going on in my head of a juve wearing a flat cap. Bone cutters came at *Flat Cap* from all angles, simultaneously, with a minimum of fuss, cutting off its arms and legs. All the while, Flat Cap, arterial spray crisscrossing its face, was happily smiling away.

The ad was digitally fresh. You could tell by the crispness of the mental picture, the lack of blurring around the subliminal. From this, you could discern that the actual op had happened only hours before. There was no pain. Alongside the blood and wet stumps, there was serenity. The only explanation was that Flat Cap was one of the first beneficiaries of a new wonder drug. What else could it be.

I didn't wait for the breakdown of pricing to follow. I shook my head and banished the images from my skull.

I continued on my way inside the store. Hanging from every wall on display pegs were plastic bags of a dark murky liquid. It was Grunge.

Open planning. The shopfloor was an estuary with several rooms branching off. You could peer in and witness a number of surgical procedures taking place.

In one room, a juve, all flashing teeth, was injected with Grunge through the upper lip. The view in real time wasn't as crystal clear as the digital ad, the naked eye couldn't be relied on to take it all in, but here, there was nothing left to the imagination. *Flashing Teeth*'s legs, just removed, were replaced by piston limbs. Busy machine parts never at peace, grinding into puffy serrated flesh.

Another room, another crude assignation. This time an arm was chopped off at the joint at the elbow. A gun barrel and accompanying joist bored into the open wound. It took two technicians standing side by side to carry out the task and push the new appendage in. The whole experience looked excruciating, and should have been so, if not for the ecstasy written large on the recipient's face. It was the type of expression you would associate with a surprise birthday party. Not a hint of screaming, or discomfort, or goddamn anything, a self-contained pleasure. The quiet was the unnerving thing. One of many.

And next door, oh brother, my old pal Buzzsaw was getting his jaw reattached.

At the far end of the shopfloor was a dope at the desk with a Nazi tattoo for a face. Typical of fascist gun-runner fleshpot cultists everywhere, it was impossible to see for all the ink if he was happy to see me.

I approached at my own pace, arms running free, undulating easily. In the name of self-preservation, my chameleon skin grafts kicked in, covering my skin in tiny swastikas, so I fitted right in.

Eyeball to eyeball, I came to an inevitable stop.

"What-you-at?" *Nazi Tattoo* asked me.

It looked up and saw, hovering over my head, having floated in along with me, the black cloud. Under the shop's strobe lighting, it was less a dormant cloud and more a waspish angry swarm.

"Neat-affection," it said.

Why was I here? I couldn't say the real reason, now could I? That there was a network of Nazis who had designed a drug that blocked the body's pain transmitters, permanently. And that drug was Grunge. It was new. It was about to dig in, attain prevalence, and with it in place, nothing to stop any Meat Spacer from amassing one bloody enhancement after another.

No pain, only gain. The advertising slogan would go.

Enhanced meat. The introduction of Grunge

would tip the balance. The more the dopes and creeps were under the influence, the more they accumulated, and the less likely they'd make the decision to pass over. Under the influence, no one would ever willingly choose to enter Godspace. A whole wretched generation lost, backs turned, dead to the possibility.

Freedom of choice may very well have been an illusion, but still, an illusion worth keeping.

Why should AI care? Why the interest unbecoming of the next evolutionary step, and giddily so? Mankind had made its bed; made peace with atrophy and extinction. So why not leave it there? A little wave, *Adios Amigo Adios My Friend*, and then poof, Godspace is gone. Becomes the stuff of myth and legend.

But Greek gods got involved in human affairs for a whole lot less. No, seriously, look at Zeus. Starting wars, punishing humanity for stealing fire. The gods followed their many carnal desires, siring many illegitimate children in the process. They had the demigods, the result of union between deity and human, and from the heights of Mount Olympus, the gods would have them do their bidding.

And this was me after a fashion. A demi-god; union of Godspace and Meat Space. And I would do Zeus's bidding. To prevent Grunge from taking root. At Ground Zero.

But I wasn't going to volunteer this type of information to the slab of meat currently facing me with a swastika for a face.

Nazi Tattoo was already bent over at the desk and sniffing at me furiously.

"Yah-coated-in-somethin'?"

There were sutured limbs everywhere. A service hatch was being lifted.

"You-Pan?"

The human race was shrinking and so was the world around them. It wasn't down to me to make things better. I just had to make sure it didn't get worse.

"Wanna-chop-chop-doo-wop-tik-tok?"

It didn't wait for an answer. Instead, a calloused hand was wrapped around my throat. Weight pushing me back, keeping me there. An emaciated sunbeam reflected on metal as Nazi Tattoo raised its other arm. Enhanced arm. Poised. There was a hook attached.

This was Threat Level three.

In response, my hands too had their own purpose. Move like lightning, reach out and snap Nazi Tattoo's neck. In one-two-three-four-two. All that was left for its broken head was to flop listlessly towards me, which allowed me to slip a tag—a teardrop button with a pulse—under the loose skin around the neck.

I sidestepped and was free of an already diminished body. It fell like a stone to the floor while I remained standing. I turned a quarter circle.

"Blow-the-freddy-frances-sky-high!"

Surprise Birthday Party from one of the procedures of before, appeared with a newly piston-powered machine gun for an arm. Entering the fray with gusto, dispensing bullets, poisoned pellets nicking the air. Rat-a-tat-tat. On repeat. Rat-a-tat-tat.

"Arghh!" it screamed. In exultation, you'd have to guess. A thimble of euphoria. "Blarghh-Blehh-Barf!"

Unleashing a hail of fatal buzzbomb wasp stings. Projectile lead. And I was the target. This was Threat Level four.

This activated a protective shield, originating from that layer of epidermis found under the outer skin. The shield pushed out, causing the bullets to bend around me.

Surprise Birthday Party was not for wavering, until he was. Something was in its line of vision, faltering. Distracted by what was left of Nazi Tattoo.

The nanites were no longer a cloud. No longer anchored, having zoned in on the pulse of the tag, devouring the organic matter it found there. Flesh, blood, all the icky germs and viruses that inhabit within, obliterating shape, nullifying existence. Surprise Birthday Party couldn't help but focus on how the nanites went about their business in straight and narrow procession. When they got to the face, following the lines of the tattoo, feasting at ninety-degree turns.

Powerless to do anything but watch, mouth open. The escalating Threat Level was enough for the nanites to remain activated and so displace the air molecules around Surprise Birthday Party. In they went through the mouth and other orifices. It was an inside job.

Slice and dice. Dissected. Piece by random piece.

Caught unawares. Surprise Birthday Party dissipated in front of me. A collective nanite energy field keeping each body part in place, as if still attached to the body, while waiting its turn.

Not comprehending its fate until it looked down. Right thigh was missing. As was the groin. Just empty space in their place. Nanites kept going, gobbling up the firing mechanism of its gun limb. An existence, however brief, without nipples. Finding it hard to swallow became impossible to swallow. No throat. Surprise Birthday Party didn't have the time to close a now lipless kisser before blinking out totally.

Immediate danger dealt with, but I wasn't out of the woods yet. Emerging from the various doorways and hidey holes came more citizens of Meat Space. The drunks and punks and flunkies. All with newly acquired enhancements: bazookas, rifles, an ArmaLite, revolvers, pistols, grenades, bayonets, hunting knives, a Claymore sword. That and Grunge flowing through their bloodstreams and sweating out their pores.

There was all kinds of noise coming out of all kinds of mouths. It formed a godawful chorus; terrible moaning that assaulted your earlobes all the way down to your gut strings. Heralding every type of extremity, demonstration of a combined destructive power sufficient to level a small town.

In among them, out sprung Flat Cap, pin-up boy, *star* of the ad that filled my senses upon entering the shop. Flat Cap with pneumatic springs for legs and shotguns for arms. Still smiling that odd, misplaced smile. With a blood-curdling *boing*, it jumped into the air. Letting off both barrels.

I ducked but didn't need to, the shots went above my head.

Flat Cap was back down, on impact with the floor, demonstrating a balletic frenetic quality you'd associate with a dope on springs. Balanced on one spring, he raised the other one, which snaked up and reloaded the shotguns. Behind it was the baying enhanced mob, about to unleash hell.

Call it Threat Level Immeasurable. Nothing to keep anything back. No-tags-required. Not any silver lining.

I needed my own brand of firepower. Bolts of lightning handed down by the gods. In the time it took for each of the mob to aim. The flutter of a single eyelid. I could be faster than time, if only for a short while.

The nanite swarm buzzed above me, twitchy, lumpen. Puppy dogs trying to find their way out of a sack. Then the tiny machines rained down on me, circling my arms, immersed in black cumulus. Mercifully quick, but that was the only mercy shown to me. They ate my arms, stripping off every shred of flesh and sinew. All the way down to the bone. I did not scream, which surprised me, instead I let out an almighty roar. The unexpected nature of this provided a distraction from the excruciating pain. If only for the few seconds it took to empty my lungs.

I thought of Athena, who was Zeus's best-loved offspring, the chosen one, his favourite demi-god. She was granted the honour of carrying the Aegis into battle, which was the breastplate of Zeus, a Gorgon's head at its centre. Athena, goddess of wisdom and war, architect of the Trojan Horse. Where Meat Space meets Godspace, through the searing pain, I thought of me.

I held out my arms in front of me, picked clean. Except they were unrecognisable, interconnecting blocks of meta-charged light metal alloy. My nano knitting needles. Citizens of Meat Space liked guns with a retro vibe which made a big noise, but not for me. I had laser rifles for arms.

And this was the scene of the crime.

Immediately, I dispensed laser fire across the mob, already stunted by the relativity of time.

I cut a swathe through the front line and right on cue, on a downward trajectory, slid chunks of sunken meat. Slapping down on the shop floor and contributing to all types of tripping hazards.

Normal time resumed. Which was time enough to seal the mob's fate. Now done with me, the nanites replicated themselves at a rate faster than speeding bullets. Rapid sentient alloy. They created a storm cloud; a roaring agglomerate that stripped both human flesh and metal appendage. The nanites had weaponized the air, and in this respect, they did not discriminate. There was nowhere to run, and they descended. They ripped the mob apart and then consumed them.

A plague of nanites which didn't stop there. Continuing through the shop, munching through anything that could be seen as a threat. The bags of

Grunge were consumed, contents eviscerated. Made into empty space and then scattered there.

The cloud, now elongated and snaking, taking on a more recognisable life of its own, located the back-room lab that distilled the Grunge. I remained on the shop floor but was granted a looksee, thanks to a psy-chic connection carried over from residual sublim-inals. It was a beatnik science lab. Basic. Quaint. In the corner a massive metal pot and three-foot long plastic stirrer. The nanites ignored these, instead focussing on shattering various tubes; gobbling up mixing and measuring equipment; causing various burners to combust. Locating and devouring hard, thumb and flash drives; same fate as liquids and pow-ders; active and inactive ingredients. And it was over. Job done. Mission completed. Ground zero now a big fat zero.

We'd reached the point where there was nothing to see. There wasn't any point in closing my eyes.

They'd had their chance. Godspace didn't come to you, you had to go to it. Only humans, or what can be loosely defined as human, could pass either way. Given the opportunity, why would anyone with a fraction of a brain want to stay in Meat Space? Pride, arrogance, stupidity? The ridiculous notion of human supremacy and the equally absurd claim for the fight against technological subjugation? Watching by as Nazis inherited the earth. Maybe I could have asked someone why this was the case, one of the locals. Not that I would take any attempt at an answer seriously.

As expected, the swastikas all over my skin as way

of disguise began to fade, even though I was left with a more permanent reminder of where I'd been and what I'd done. Mesh for arms.

A bead of sweat trailed down my forehead, gaining speed as it followed the curve of the bridge of my nose. I was so weary. My burden had grown so heavy. I was so ready to return to where I came from.

Still, I couldn't stop myself from thinking furiously. This was only a lab, you needed factories to mass produce the stuff. Maybe there had been more lotteries, resulting in more of the likes of me on the ground. It made sense. All kinds of individuals passing over the threshold of Godspace to take out all aspects of Grunge production that had popped up across the city and surrounding areas. In so doing, nullifying the threat, restoring free thought at the expense of tyranny. I didn't truly know. I wasn't told anything of the sort. And why should they tell me anything anyway? Need to know. I tried to slow my thoughts down, conscious of the clawing paranoia grappling at my soul. Infected already by the city around me. It was even more imperative that I go in and do my job, efficiently, brutally, and then get the hell out.

In the aftermath, the nanites emerged from the lab like rumbling thunder; agitated, electric, unbearably heavy, a devourer of space. The space within space. To swarm around me on the shop floor. It fell to me to calm them down again. There was no one else but me.

A sudden thought; a hope that this was not a realisation. I had to lead the way. They had to enable me to lead the way. Where I led, they would follow. Did they see me as a threat? Even though that part of me they'd see as a danger was made by them? The equivalent of being hoisted by their own petard? My own petard not far behind.

You let the internal logic transcend you, otherwise it would tie you in knots.

Twinkle, twinkle, little star

Tendrils of tiny stars coalesced and wrapped around my arms and chest—inciting all-too-human reactions, head pounding, bones aching, choking, coughing—feeding on my sweat as way of a starter. The main course; they dug underneath my skin and devoured my protective shield.

How I wonder what you are

Now, I closed my eyes, which made no discernible difference because I could no longer see. The swarm had eaten my eyes.

No Threat Level here

The last remnants of a psychic link. The dying embers of a mind slowly twinkling out.

And so, I waited for the final squeeze, inside and out, that would take me into oblivion. *There was no one else but...*

I just wanna go home

Stripped of the capacity to communicate with them or to think something, surrounded as I was by an atrocity of emptiness. The threat of Grunge-making Nazi organ leggers dealt with, and now there was nothing else. And I was so very tiny.

The nanites switched themselves off. They became

something less than dust, never to be reactivated, and instead be caught in the streams of nearby air conditioners and blasted into the ether where they would climb and climb and be displaced, and eventually mix with the microscopic remnants of stars long dead.

Hopefully, I'd done enough. It would qualify as the greater good. Grunge eradicated at the source. No further action required. And if this proved not to be the case, they would raise another lottery and send someone else in for another sweep. But not me.

Hurt all over. The body parts that remained, the ones no longer there. For now, I stood and screamed the pain out of me. All the frustration and indignity, and identity. And I did so until…

Nothing.

I was blind, and my internal GPS was on its last legs. I made for the main door. The ad, again, featuring an intact Flat Cap—it was all relative—reared up in my head, but I was in no mood to stick around. I stumbled out of the flesh store, then the mall itself. I was in a daze. I clung to the hope that nothing would try to stop and eviscerate me. Attempt to pluck out my organs and wring them dry, creating pools of gunk that gathered at their feet wherever they should roam. I could be that lucky.

Outside, seeking out the coolness of shadows was instinctive. That I steered clear of the open vents. I was gripped with the irrational fear that if I tipped one way, the buildings around me would follow suit. And everything would be falling, sliding off the edge of the world into an endless abyss of damage and self-repair. That at the bottom waiting for us all was a sea of skulls and rotten bones. The denial of heaven. There'd be no way back.

When I first laid sight on them I never trusted my legs, and now they were all I had. I did not lean and I did not bend. I kept my hold on a dying, shrinking world and wondered aloud, "What have you to offer me?"

"Where-yah-at?" came the unlikely reply. I followed the sound of the wheezing which accompanied it.

Big One was still on the ground where I had left it. There was something different, the scent of red about it, indicating it had made a recent kill. I'd almost forgotten what it was to eat. But not so being eaten.

"The mall," I said.

"Yah-get-your-arms?"

I lifted my two laser rifles from either side. "Something like that," I said, with something that resembled a smile. Pardon my French. *Bras doubles.*

"Yar-stink…"

"Yes, my stink…"

On the long, ragged walk over, my capacity to think returned to me. I could not see, but I could adapt if I was here long enough, which I wouldn't be. My arms throbbed with pulsar energy. Harnessing the power of a nanite-sized sun, I had on my person sufficient capability to wipe out what was left of the miserable human race. I could have started with Big One. Just aim and think. Conventionally-sized laser fire. Conventionally-seized laser fire. But that would imply the desire to reduce everything to molecular ashes, and I wasn't that kind of person. I parked the thought for now.

"No-tatts…"

"Yes, no tatts…"

There wasn't much point putting up the pretence anymore. In the little time I'd been here I'd grown weary of this plane. There was no hiding the fact I dreamed of ascension.

"Whas-it-like?" Big One asked. "The-place-beyond?"

"It is the Fluidity," I said. "It is Godspace. Heaven. Nirvana. Olympus. As names go, I don't have a preference.

"You can be everywhere. Think about it, if you want to. All at once. You can be at the centre of a nascent star. You can be twenty-seven back in the dark ages buying your first vinyl. Be surrounded by the sound of breathing. It can be so incredibly peaceful. You need never think another regular thought again.

"We're not human anymore, but we can be more human than we ever thought possible. None of the limitations apply. We soar, we literally soar. A higher form of evolution that never overwhelms or discriminates, unless that's what you want.

"The world comes to you," I continued. "You don't need to go search for it. And it is a perfect world, not the grimy grungy counterfeit place waiting for you at the end of the street outside your room. Cut adrift of your workstation. For there lies a world of disappointment and pain, the so-called real world. Grimy, dirty, cluttered with discarded plastic bags and dogshit.

"In the same vicinity as other people, strangers. Never to make eye contact for fear they snatch away your soul. This is what happens when you walk away from heaven.

"And all those moments lost along the way. All those chances missed."

It began to shuffle. Evidence of laboured movement. "One-hand-flat-on-the-ground-push-up-to-the-knees," it said. "I-soar."

At best, I could put my arms behind my back. The weight, the strain, around my body was everything. "You listening? You understand?" I said, "I can't see, not thinking straight. There is no Godspace anywhere. It won't reveal itself to me."

"Yah-think-yah-got-it-bad? Up-top.

"Yah-see-it?"

"What?" Face turned up, pulling back my cervical spine as far as my neck could muster. Another pointless act to grace an increasingly futile existence. "I can't see. What do you mean?"

There was no light. As clear as Grunge.

And then, it was clear to me; even to my hollow sockets for eyes. I could still form a pattern in my mind's eye. Could sense it because it had always been there on high. Couldn't see heaven, though.

Up in the sky, a big neon arrow pointing back down at me.

FACE OF THE CITY

Charlie had intense blue eyes. There was little he could not do with those eyes. Little he could not see. His face was effortlessly contoured; strong chin, cheekbones sublimely inclined, a picture of perfect symmetry.

He was dressed in an immaculately white shirt. An affectation bestowed on him by his *dresser* droids. He held a smart tweed jacket so it dangled easily over his back and shoulder. His other arm engaged in a swagger-friendly, karate-like movement. As smooth as marble. He was made that way. He couldn't help himself. He struck a pose.

He was surrounded by floating bubble droids, each to a machine wearing Homburg hats. Their slender robot arms carried vintage graphic cameras with flash bulbs, which went off one after the other. A quickening of the pulse. A snap of the fingers. The roll of a drum. This was typical of a photo shoot, at least for the city. The city where Charlie was its face.

'Smile Charlie smile' emitted one of the droids.

A spread the arms, nonchalant, a swirling motion, and the jacket was now on him. Two droids descended with garment brushes held in spindly robotic hands. One concentrated on the top of the jacket, the other started at the bottom, working down, working up, and meeting at the middle.

Charlie smiled and posed some more, knuckles under the chin. There was a fresh series of flashes, creating a ring of photons, porous fireflies; a pop-pop-pop.

Charlie was not only the face of the city; he was the reason too.

An urban expanse with all the trimmings. On the end of flag posts erected across Midtown. Concentrated at the intersection. Charlie's face adorned every advertising board and giant TV screen affixed to every tall building and skyscraper. It was his smile—it was his pose—on repeat, like a pattern, a motif, sculpted into the city itself.

Every building was unoccupied but fastidiously maintained. And it was sunny. A clear sky.

The photoshoot now ended, Charlie took a walk outside to catch a breath and take a vape. At any one time, looking up through puffs of purple smoke, he would spy several hov-cabs fly by.

Charlie removed his jacket which he again held over his shoulder. A bubble droid wearing a beanie hat buzzed around him. The droids were all linked to the city intelligence and there was nothing they wouldn't do for him.

'Let me hold your jacket for you' *Beanie Hat* said.

"No, it's all cool," Charlie said.

He used his spare hand to shield the sun from his eyes before raising it to hail a passing hov-cab. It didn't matter which one.

A cab in the air—with added steel bumpers to lend it character—glided towards him.

The driver, consisting of a synthetic waist, moveable arms, torso, head, and wearing a fez, stuck its head out of the open driver-side window.

'What a great photo shoot' the driver said. 'Took the liberty of tuning in

'You are in and you are out bada-boom bada-voom bada-ding'

Charlie eased into the front and only passenger seat.

'Where to boss the usual'

"The usual." Charlie leaned forward and adopted an earnest expression, which he liked to think of as his default one. "The edge of the city."

The hov-cab flew over the metropolis below, passing a dome-like conurbation on the left and a sprawling medical lab on the right.

Rather like the vehicle he piloted; the cab driver's voice box was in full flight. 'Just passed *City Intelligence* and further on get a load of *The Fountain* keeping everything fresher than fresh and bubbly'

Throughout the city, there was evidence of construction. Despite the incessant activity, which was 24/7, its streets and buildings remained clean and pristine. There was no dust. The city made use of everything.

The city was constantly changing without seeming to actually change. In a moment of self-reflection, the facade Charlie had constructed with meticulous care around him slipped. He wondered if the monotony of existence would ever stop. The city was stifling him. The illusion of change.

By keeping him alive the city was killing him.

Having reached his destination, Charlie stood on a strip of tarmac at the city's edge. He was joined by another droid wearing another beanie hat, or maybe it was the same one as before. All that lay in front of them, beyond the city borders, was smouldering irradiated wasteland.

'What could you possibly need out here Charlie' it asked.

"Some hush, maybe?"

He looked out with another of his trademark expressions; the achingly wistful one. He gazed at the shimmer that demarcated the city's edge. Even here, there was further evidence of construction. Several buzzing bubble droids with hard hats, strategically deploying their tractor fields, busied themselves moving a heavy girder.

As it transpired, some hush was not what Charlie wanted after all.

"Can you see it?" he asked suddenly. There was no response.

"The city, pooft." He puffed out his to-die-for lips. "Ever-growing, pushing out its boundaries, buildings on buildings, and every day I go to the edge.

"Not that any of you tell me anything. I have to do this for myself.

"More in hope than anything, but I do it anyway. I forget about the city, surrounded by endless wasteland, and I search for signs of life."

And then, gushing through him, tumultuous, like a river breaking its banks after heavy rainfall, was a sense of longing. It was acute and sincere and without bounds. Charlie looked beyond the skyline, past the pinched atmosphere, squinting perfect eyes, to the point he could make out the suggestion of intermittent stars winking back down at him.

"I can't be the only one left.

"Can I really be alone in the universe? It seems so meaningless and pointless. Is it so wrong to hope to find someone somewhere that could live with me in the city?

"I mean, there is so much room."

There was a pressure inside him. A sharp, byzantine, screeching heat. He held his left arm.

Beanie hat circled him in a flurry of ellipses.

'Something is wrong' it said.

"My arm hurts!"

Shooting pain, an upsurge of molten blood, broke out of his chest, extending to the tips of his fingers. He was no longer on his feet.

'Ohmyohnomyohmy' Beanie Hat's movements became even more erratic. It had lost its centre.

Close by, the *Hard Hats*, having dropped the girder, sped towards the scene.

'Charlie we need to get you to'

The Fountain. Consistent of transparent tubular tanks, one after the other, linked together by sections of living tissue, stretching as far as the eye, synthetic or otherwise, could see. Occupying each of the tanks, or at least the ones that mattered, were faint humanoid shapes enveloped in various states of viscous muddy liquid. All the necessary parts were there but some of the body shapes were irregular, not entirely joined up.

A multitude of droids wearing scrub caps traversed the area. Regularly checking temperature gauges and bio-readings and oxygen levels, bobbing up and down among the tanks, blurring the lines, creating a kinetic hypnotic wave of elasticity.

The city was bustling once. Teeming with people on people on people. It was an impurity at first, passing between them, invisible to the naked eye. Mostly harmless. Then it changed in the most radical way imaginable. It became a silent assassin. And it ripped through the city population, save only one. After such a virulent, drawn-out onslaught, only Charlie came out the other side and exhibited signs of immunity.

That was an eternity ago, or so it seemed to Charlie in the less lucid moments, but what was clear was that the air went bad and everyone died, except for Charlie. The city salvaged what body parts and organs it could and stored them in the facility known as The Fountain.

There was one prominent tank, taking central position, besieged by oxygenated bubbles. Inside was Charlie, as naked as the day he was born. There was a hole in his chest where his heart should be. Sticking out, circling the contours of the cavity, were several metal wires, flexing in unison.

The city wanted—no, a crucial and strategic piece of code at the core of City Intelligence in fact, needed—a living, organic figurehead. A city without people was unthinkable. Without person. And here

Charlie fitted the bill seamlessly. But the original Charlie was not built to last.

A matter of routine, Charlie was maintained, replenished and rebuilt where necessary utilising the contents of the tubular megaliths of the Fountain.

Made animate. A collection of bits.

A precedent set. And this was how this fragile body of his, itself the latest in a series of iterations, received the care it required. Both cosmetic and medical. The science of rejuvenation.

Back at the tank, a panel slid open at Charlie's feet. From there, a fully functioning heart, propelled through the pipes, sashayed into the tank. Up it skooshes. The wires in Charlie's chest there to meet it. To cradle it. To take it to his bosom. Everything in place, the heart burrowed into him. To initiate a warm wetness, a wholeness, a wellness. To take up its rightful position. A spark in the alkaline fired up the neural matter and air bubbles escaped from his mouth. And Charlie was as good as new.

Just like the city.

*

A new heart, a new day. A military transport aircraft entered city airspace. A small plane. A plane that brought *him* to Charlie, and things would never be the same.

But before everything changed, a fully recovered Charlie stood in the city square with a Beanie hat-garlanded droid for company.

The square, elegant and spacious with a red asphalt concourse, opened up in front of Charlie. Occupying the centre of the square was a Prosopis cineraria tree, resplendent in green leaves, which stood over thirty feet high. It was the only tree of its size growing in the city. Often referred to as *The Tree of Life*. And he loved that tree; liked to think it would love him back if it could.

Bronze statues, inward-facing, showing no signs of corrosion or oxidation, lined the perimeter of the square. Every statue was in the shape of a person, demonstrating a period of humanity over the ages—medieval, Middle Ages, industrial, World War. Each figure cast in supplication, many with their hands held in the air.

Normally, Charlie would mingle between the statues and stare at the tree for hours. It was enough for him to know it was growing, even though, obviously, he could not see it happening before his eyes. But the knowledge of this granted him inner peace, if only for a short time.

In times of serenity, he could come to terms with what he was, and with what he wasn't.

But today was different. His mind was on other things. The grin on his face stretched from ear to ear. His body was shaking. He couldn't hide his excitement, even if he wanted to. As way of contrast, Beanie Hat swayed from side to side in agitation.

'Please Charlie' it said, 'you should go indoors'

"Are you crazy?" he said. "The plane might be manned. There might be people!"

On the march, having appeared from the opposite side of the square, were four marines. Dressed in reflective camouflage kit, advancing in a set pattern. The marines wore gas masks, chest bags, their rifles aimed.

'We need to go Charlie' Beanie Hat screeched. 'We need to go now'

Charlie stood transfixed by their approach. It took all his self-control not to hold out his arms in welcome.

He wanted so much to embrace another human being. Something with a pulse. Something with blood running in their veins.

Instead, Charlie dropped to his knees and held up his arms as a way of surrender. He was as still and as submissive as the statues in the square.

Beanie Hat continued to hover around him, its movements as erratic as it could muster. 'Charlie are you sure about this sweet child you are not thinking straight'

Charlie stared at the droid's plating and saw a facsimile of a reflection staring back at him. Spitting feathers. "They are marines!" he said.

'Not marines

'Not any longer'

A volley of fire smacked into Beanie Hat's plating, leaving their mark, a pitted surface. The force of the shots caused the machine to spin and career wildly. It dipped and scraped along the ground as it made its escape.

"On your knees!" a marine hollered.

"I'm with you!" Charlie replied, already down on his knees.

"Just do it!"

"I'm doing it! It's done!"

"Hands in the air!"

Even though his arms were cramping, Charlie looked up to confirm his hands were indeed in the air. "Can't you see?"

The marines were close, all four screaming at him from different vantage points. Charlie just got hotter and more confused as a consequence, and his knees, which had never left the ground, were beginning to hurt.

There was a pleading intensity in his eyes. Another affectation.

"No need for guns, please…"

The marines walked past the Tree of Life. One of them couldn't tear his gaze away from it. The marine in question got down on one knee and lowered his weapon to the floor.

"Pelton, what are you doing?" a fellow marine asked.

"He's surrendering," Pelton said. "He's not a threat."

"I repeat—what are you doing?"

"I repeat—"

Laser beams shot out from adjacent statues, slicing on impact, effortlessly, reducing uniformed flesh and bone into chunks of inert meat.

The one exception was the crouched Pelton, a beam glancing his forehead, taking a lump of skull with it. But for all that, and unlike his three comrades, his frame now on the ground, wounded, but body virtually intact.

Charlie watched on aghast. All Charlie remembered was the city, and even so, he still found it full of surprises. Riven with adrenaline, fragmented by shock, and without a thought for himself, Charlie ran towards the melee.

He found marine Pelton, having somehow turned on his back, head now shaped like an apostrophe mark, choking on blood flowing from his wound, seeping into his gas mask. His fingers grappled uselessly with the straps of the mask, emitting a noise like a faulty air vent that might be taken for breathing.

"The air will kill you," said Charlie.

Pelton continued to grapple with the mask.

Charlie crouched down, couldn't stand by and do nothing, helped Pelton loosen his mask, made slippy with blood. Fragments of the other man's skull lodged under his fingernails as a result. The mask fell away and the man underneath could have been Charlie: same age, same eyes, perhaps even a similar situation. Both of them were trapped, in their own particular way.

The marine had a crewcut. He had none of Charlie's curls.

He struggled for breath. Charlie got down on his back, slid under Pelton to offer what little comfort he could.

"The droids will bring help," Charlie said.

"No droids," the marine said.

Charlie tried to look away. Tried not to focus on

the gaping hole that used to be the top of the marine's head.

"Holy shit," Charlie said.

"That bad, huh?" The marine's voice was so quiet, it barely registered as a whisper. But then again, there was no kind of background noise to drown it out; there was only Charlie.

"I have my orders…" Pelton raised a hand, trying unsuccessfully to stop it shaking. "…the resources, logistics, it took to get us here, ughh, to destroy the City Intelligence."

A single beat.

"Don't you know this?" the marine asked. But Charlie did not know how to react. Or answer. His tongue felt like it had doubled in size in his mouth.

"You know this," the marine answered for him. "City Intelligence exploits a loophole in the global grid. To keep you alive, the only living person-cough- in the city. This circumvents all other priorities. What's left of the NSA can't find a way around it.

"The city is growing exponentially, draining the planet's power supply. If this goes on, uh, listen, there won't be a world anymore. Only the city, nothing else. You understand? It will all be gone.

"You need to help us. Damnit—Charlie—won't you help us?"

Charlie was stunned by this. He didn't quite under-stand what was expected of him, and yet the marine's words confirmed what he knew to be true already. That his existence up to this point was sterile and vacuous. Deprived of purpose. Sucking the life out of the world. There was a feeling in the pit of his stomach; a debilitating, coruscating one. That resident in Charlie's gut was the overriding compulsion that he wanted to make a difference. It's just that he'd never had the opportunity before.

"Yes," he said.

"Yes, yes."

Pelton's eyes could no longer focus. He was losing awareness of who he was, but still, his orders were ingrained, imprinted on him. The pain from the crack on his head grew exponentially, getting bigger, moving down, threatening to cut him in two. Adrenaline couldn't keep the full reality of his situation at bay forever.

Despite this, because of this, he continued. "You see it, the chest bag. Inside is a device. Do your duty, you take it, get inside City Intelligence, enter the digits 2424. That's what it takes to prime it -cough- then you have twenty seconds to get yourself clear."

"OK, I understand."

Charlie didn't really understand, but knew he was in the grip of something much bigger than himself. Something unbelievably important. That fate would be his guiding hand.

"I think I do."

Something coursing through him. A feeling of duty. Pumping oxygen directly into the brain. Cometh the hour.

"You need to breathe."

They were together and he could feel him breathing, and twitching. His chest was moving and that's all that mattered. Charlie adjusted and wrapped his arms around the marine. He was as light as a feather.

"Stay with me. Please…"

Charlie was aware of the blood on his hands. And on his clothes. The marine was bleeding out, on top of him, bleeding into him. He could feel the presence of the Tree of Life behind him—behind *them*. That the tree was all about symbolism. Charlie had always been aware. Life had to be cherished. Without life, what else was there? And now this was his chance to make good on this.

There was a shudder, the suggestion of a rattle. Pelton lay still in his arms.

And then there was only him. There had always been him.

Charlie knew that the city would take everything. What was left of the fallen marines would be scooped up and processed. Organs; the base materials—blood, flesh, bone—would be separated and broken down. Even the dried blood in Charlie's clothes would be reconstituted. Nothing would go to waste.

That would happen soon enough, but Charlie didn't plan to be around when it did.

"I need to breathe." He pushed himself up into a crouching position, cradling the chest bag.

"I'm sorry." He took out the device.

'What is that in your hand Charlie'

"It's a joke."

After the carnage of the square, Charlie, bedraggled, fettered by the weight of a forbidden world on his shoulders, stumbled his way towards the domelike conurbation that was City Intelligence. This was the heart of the city, the beating heart, its quickened pulse.

And Charlie had eyes only for it.

En route, there was nothing but concrete and steel. Charlie encountered no droids, nothing in the sky, nothing on the ground. The city had sucked the life out of him. Turning him inside out. Exposing a poison running through his veins. It had shaped him into something he did not recognise. And he'd stood there, and allowed it to cosset and infantilise him, and let it happen. But no longer.

Inside, Charlie stood in front of a giant projected face. Giant, green, fluorescent, surrounded by fire, and all for Charlie's benefit.

'What type of joke Charlie' it said.

Charlie held up the device, appropriated from the marine, high above his head. It was an innocuous square box with a now redundant keypad. He had already primed the bomb.

The feeling simmering inside him was a mix of regret, remorse and defiance. Decision already made even before entering the building.

All lit up. The device made a beep.

"As if you don't know," Charlie said. "You could have put a stop to me anywhere, at any time.

"You made mincemeat of the soldiers. You've already taken what's left of them. Stuffed in vacuum-sealed bags.

"What have I done, have I ever achieved, except live when everyone else has died?"

The face of City Intelligence glitched momentarily, then the portrayal of anguish. The fire got brighter.

'No' it said, 'do not say that do not think that'

"My choice." Charlie held out the device in both hands as if to make an offering. As if played out, some age-old religion. As if to worship the sun.

"This is what I am," he said. "This is who I am."

The sound that came from the bomb was now continuous. —*beepbeepbeepbeep*—

'Charlie we only want you to be happy to run free to be loved to be adored

'You are the world to us'

There was thunder taking shape in Charlie's ears, cut short as the building was engulfed in mushroom cloud. And more besides.

Leaving in its wake another gaping hole. This time, it was the city.

*

Charlie was nowhere.

And at the same time, Charlie was everywhere.

Reduced to dust by the explosion and carried by the wind, in this way he entered every pore of the city.

There was time. It took time. Cascading down, the levels of radiation exposure.

A visor-wearing bubble droid hovered above ground zero. The ground below was flattened and moribund. It amounted to a blast radius of a kilometre.

A third of the city was either wiped out or its infrastructure severely compromised, and much in the way of rebuilding was to be done.

The droid descended, produced then placed a beaker in the dirt, and took a sample.

The fatal flaw was to assume that City Intelligence was consigned to a single building, a sole location. That City Intelligence wasn't anything other than the city itself.

The droid lifted up the beaker to best examine the dirt sample. It searched for a spark, no matter how minuscule, no matter how statistically insignificant. It searched for nothing at all.

It would not sit well to merely dismiss the raid as a futile gesture. The marines had their orders. If this was to be humanity's last stand, then this fact alone served to give it meaning. There was always something left behind. And it's not as if all of this hadn't happened before.

Where were the droids on that fateful day when Charlie took matters into his own hands and sought to sacrifice everything? They flew the coop, shifted outside the blast radius, and took with them as many of the constituents of the Fountain as they could. Never to think to let him in on it.

Now there was another Fountain, makeshift, ragged around the edges, but nothing some applied engineering wouldn't fix. And—

Back to the Fountain, then; one tank in particular, where the droid activity around it would be best described as frantic. From a distance, it could be mistaken for flying ants working furiously, dedicated to replenishing the hive. Through the murkiness, adjoining parts came together to form a recognisable shape. A comforting outline.

Body parts come together, filling dead space, animating what once was inert. Rising up from the murk.

The concept of rebuild was not alien. But to make sense of this, the city needed a sense of purpose. It needed a reason. Without such a thing, how could anything hope to go on forever?

Another set of flashes, one after the other, pop-pop-pop. Nerve ends dancing in unison, moving arms, kicking legs. Bubbles escaping from the mouth. It wasn't an easy birth, but it was a joyous one, worthy of a photo shoot.

'Smile Charlie smile'

*

Baby steps transitioning into something firmer. And later, all dressed up with somewhere to go, he would find himself once more at the edge of the city.

Pelton would be there, too. Often, he would imagine he was standing in the marine's boots. In the marine's skin. And that they were constant companions, peering up at the thinning sky, contented by the assurance of the infinity of space and the certainty of universes coming together.

Sometimes he wore a gas mask and other times he did not.

But at all times he would strut his stuff and dress

immaculately; smile, teeth, eyes, jaw, cropped hair, he looked the business.

At the city's edge, he would ask, "Can you see it?" and the reply that would surely come: 'Yes Charlie I can see it all'

The face of the city.

THE INSIGNIFICANCE OF TIME TRAVEL

I scoop up another one with impossible care, as if the spoon is holding something incredibly hollow and fragile, like a world or a universe. But it's neither of these. I take the flake and pop it in my mouth. I swish it from one side of my mouth to the other. Even though my saliva does its job, reducing it quickly to a form of mush, I'm in no hurry to swallow. A residue of corn circulates my mouth. The taste is so powerful it engages my senses. I swear I can smell the cut grain, see the field the corn grew in, feel the sun beating down, the key to it all.

When I first lived this moment, I probably wolfed down the cereal. In all probability, I did so while standing, the idea of breakfast an entirely functional one. A thin layer of soya milk. Get the food down with a minimum of fuss, a minimum of everything. But now, this latest precise time, everything is different. Is so much more heightened. I'm almost giddy with excitement as I sit at the table savouring every last morsel. My face taut with anticipation. Literal crumbs of comfort. Because I know right now, we share the same world. They are still with me.

There is only one direction of time travel that I'm invested in. You go back in time. You do so not as a separate entity, but as an adjunct. On arrival, you form an additional layer which you wrap around all the layers that preceded it. You are a ghost, haunting your former self.

I'm brushing my teeth with an electric toothbrush. I catch my reflection in the mirror on the side cabinet and I find myself shaping my mouth into a little forced smile. I notice the folds of skin which catapult from my cheekbones. I can't see my lips for the foam of the toothpaste. I'll take this as my cue to stop soon.

I've been back here, oh, what seems like a thousand times. I have a name for each tooth. The furthest out, the bottom left molar, to give one example, is called Albert. My right incisor is Victoria. Maybe one day I'll group them closer together, but I've never claimed to be a Royalist so the present arrangement suits me fine. In the past, at the time, like most things I considered it a perfunctory act; one you wanted done quickly. But now I'm back, this one more time, I slow it down. I savour the sheer ordinariness and sterile mundanity of it. Every Albert. Every Victoria.

I can't control my past, I'm a ghost after all, but my future voice adds to the other voices which compete like hungry chicks inside my head. My mother, my best friend, my anxiety, my awkwardness, my natural optimism, my present and future self. And sometimes it's the latter that breaks through to exert a little influence and slow things down, and extend the time I take to brush my teeth.

Frank-Susie-Matilda-Boris-Marmaduke…

I feel guilty I haven't hoovered in a week. The oven still needs to be cleaned and the blinds straightened. I apply a form of domestic triage, which results in first emptying the dishwasher.

Behind me… I have tried so many times to blot it out, reluctantly, painfully, realising the futility of it, but ignoring this all the same. There is a phone on a kitchen surface. Its presence is suffocating. It is everywhere. It could just as well be a brick on my chest, crushing the life out of me.

But for now, the dishwasher is the thing. What else to do but start with the mugs and cutlery before moving on to the bigger stuff: plates, pots, a casserole dish with a dogged stain that should necessitate another cycle.

I think the machine needs some TLC; more detergent. A little cleansing.

Something is wrong, something begins to stir inside, the gestation of an alarm bell, and I know it won't be long before it's so oppressive I can't stand it. Even the contents of a dishwasher can't go on forever.

It's not as if I can change anything—achieve anything of any importance. I can't pick up the phone any earlier than I did a thousand times before. Only in my mind. I can't pay it no heed. These devices are designed not to be ignored.

Wasps are making their way into the house. Attracted by the ripened apples on the tree in the back garden. The wasps seem sluggish themselves. Short and erratic, intrinsically pointless flight paths.

As much of a nuisance to themselves as any other. I think they must be dying too.

The weather report reverberates from the radio. A warning of flash floods is the crux of it.

Even though I go back in time again and again, I can't change anything. Can't pick up the phone, or text. I can't get them to take the left-hand lane. Cut their speed to below seventy, under sixty, to stop driving. To just *stop*. I can't change this. These are fixed points. Unalterable and undeniable. Bolstered by the bulwark of time. Nudging over the speed limit.

The Tesco delivery man arrives later than expected. Although this would imply he'd ever arrived on time previously. I know in my heart that the big bag of pasta, soap powder, box of eggs, a packet of fruit winders, assorted frozen meals—the memories contained in his plastic delivery cart—will prove overwhelming, but I have no choice but to get through this.

I'd always considered people with a pasta-making kit to be deeply eccentric. I mean, come on, why go through the hassle when so readily available at a supermarket near you? But now, with the various food shortages and cost of living crises, one after another, I'm starting to see them as visionary.

I'm just processing. I go back in time and move from one self-contained period to another. I'm constrained and I can't go back too far. These are the moments offered up to me, and I relive them again and again.

In the kitchen, I didn't properly turn off the tap.

Sometimes I don't notice the tap leaking. Other times, it feels like each drop falls with shuddering momentum, crashing against the surface of the sink, causing the fixture and fittings to shake. I rationalise it. It's like time knows I'm here and I've outstayed my welcome.

Drip, drip, drip…

Everything is churning up inside me. I don't want to think of how things are, even though I know I can't escape it forever. The reality of the situation. The finality of things.

I move to the living room, surrounded by family photos. I need to cling on to the reality of the current situation. That's why I'm here after all. I can feel the heat, I can still feel the warmth. A discarded jacket. As best I can, while still maintaining a normal distance, I breathe it in, I taste it. I want to take off my shoes and feel the carpet under my feet and imagine the footsteps, all the impressions made by their feet. My future voice urges my past self to eat the contents of the house. For something like posterity. And of course, such a thought, such a deranged impulse, is roundly ignored.

It is oppressive. The moment of truth is far too close now. Choked with pregnant pauses, words lost and swallowed. The phone will light up and vibrate with an intensity that will cause it to jump up from the kitchen surface and move in a circular motion. Petulant child. Crying baby. It will not be ignored. A noise which has its origins from the very base of me, rising through my body, carried in my bloodstream.

The end result, a shriek that is barely human. Everything will be stripped from me. My identity, my mind.

I fold a sheet. Iron out a crease. I go upstairs and straighten the shoes below their beds so they sit perfectly aligned side by side. To go back to the start. To begin the cycle again, before it becomes too much to bear and everything breaks down again. Down, tumbling back down, I reach for the phone and steal myself.

I...

Oh god, I...

Please, I...

...scoop up another flake and pop it in my mouth. As I swish, propelling food morsels from one side of my mouth to the other, the taste of corn infiltrates my senses. I breathe in the pollen, feel the corn stretch in the cob, caught in a light rainfall, the key to it all.

Another flake, but something is different and I find I'm crouched down at the knees, my hands covering my ears. The crunch of the cornflake is too loud this time, deafening, and my teeth feel like they're conspiring against me, that they are no longer mine. Time is moving fast now, too fast. And I begin to run from my own memory. Reality around me begins to *crunch*.

Against my better judgement, I close my eyes. And when I open them...

Still crouching, but now I'm in a dimly lit tunnel. I can hear the soft thrum of machinery, originating from inside the walls, which gives the impression the tunnel is breathing.

There is another light. A stronger one at the end of the tunnel and it lends the corridor a focal point. Grants it some meaning. It is the shape of reality, the natural way of things regardless. It is everything my senses require. So I stand straight and walk towards the light. The light is a metallic teal when I really look at it. There is an air of defiance on my face, or that is the intention.

"Send me back," I say.

A voice comes from the teal. An even voice, devoid of inflection. 'Carol Estrada' it says, 'one has used up their allotted time displacement

'One has reached a limit the algorithm would never have predicted one to reach'

"Send me back."

'Time travel was intended to help one unravel issues and problems

'The intention is to help one move forward not continually bounce around in the past

'Not to be imprisoned in one's memories'

"Send me back, send me back, send me back."

'Carol Estrada we cannot help you'

The crunch of the flakes, the spikiness of toothpaste, the leaking of a tap, the vibration of a wasp's wings. This was home to me. The only things that made sense. This, I had to make the teal understand.

But when I try to speak, to find the right words to express how I truly feel, I discover they do not exist. I cannot talk.

'We cannot help you'

"It's not enough," I eventually stumble out.

'Please explain'

"It's not enough to get lost in the moment. Sometimes I can persuade myself that even the impossible is real. Is that so wrong? I repeat—I go back—one ordinary thing after another. I breathe it in—that's all I want—anything but the reality…

"The truth."

'Travelling back in time is not the answer'

"The truth takes my family away."

'Carol Estrada' There is a pause even from the teal.

"I know that's not the answer. I don't want time travel," I say.

"I want it to stop."

*

It is not as if living software ever chooses to stop when faced with a problem. It simply engineers the next stage.

The next level.

Now, for me, all the realities and pockets of time coexist. Time hasn't stopped, it has become fluid to the point of self-referential, self-fulfilling, self-aware, and I have effectively merged with time. The many, many moments, the drab and the commonplace, I am part of them, all of them. They are with me constantly.

Emerging from a single point, like a prism. Gateways to the past.

I eat cornflakes and empty the dishwasher and straighten shoes. I fold clothes and put away bags of pasta and brush my teeth. I watch wasps while listening to the weather report. I listen to the weather report while watching wasps.

In random fashion, I transition from one to the other at my leisure. Order is not important here. I can stretch time and do not exist outside of this.

And my mind accepts this; in my heart, I know it to be true. They are on the road. They are coming home. These are the moments I keep my family alive. There is a happiness to be found, distilled and trapped in time.

Insignificant to some.

My name is Carol Estrada. Mother, wife, ghost. I am the first of my kind, and I could be the last as well, for all I know. You can choose to remember me if this is acceptable to you. Or forget about me, that is no matter. But there are moments, and there is contentment.

And this is a life worth living.

EIGHT SECONDS FROM HUMAN

Deep, deep space, for there was no other kind. A medium-sized spaceship with a medium-sized name traversed a medium-sized plot of deep space. The ship was called *Altair*.

On its approach, half-thrusters on, the good ship Altair penetrated a ring of dust, helping along the space debris which broke up against its weaved titanium plating.

This was a one-man ship, or more in line given the technology involved, of one man *and* ship. Its sole passenger was a man with a medium-shaped head.

Inside, a metallic voice chirruped. 'Wake up now'

Magnus, who was lying on his back on a space mattress, stirred; was in the process of waking up. Numerous tubes and wiring were attached to his not-inconsiderable frame. He wore a fully infused Lycra body suit.

'We have reached the belt' the ship continued. Of all the voice settings Magnus could have gone for, he went for the most metallic sounding one; the most *robot*. Emotional content and timing all stripped away and replaced by a synthetic echo. He didn't have time for airs and graces. He liked to know where everything around him stood.

All in all, this latest expedition would involve three months out and the same back. He hoped in his absence his family would continue their existential prayer sessions, where they would writhe around in the floor, screaming until they could scream no more, berating themselves for having the temerity to exist in the first place. He found that a daily dose of self-loathing and nihilism was good for the soul.

His family had wept tears on the day of his departure.

For now, he sat up with a start, shrugging off the nausea. As he did so, the tubes fell away from him. For two weeks he had been in susp-an. Over the duration, his body had been pumped with a cocktail of steroids, vits and stims. As soon as awake, there was not a moment to spare. A need to be alert, toned and sharp. He needed to move, explode into action. He made it past the unisex sign just in time. And into the cubicle.

As he sat on the pan, his body suit stripped down and wrapped around his legs, stomach cramping. As he grimaced, bearing a full set of teeth, he cogitated on the weakness of the human spirit. He ruminated on the frailties of flesh and bone.

His guts erupted. An all-too-human gas nebula. Gripping the sidebars astride of him as if life depended, in the process of evacuating two weeks' worth of high cocktail intake, the veins bulged on his forehead. For someone as toned as him, someone his size, it made for an even more unedifying spectacle. In the time it took for it all to come gushing out.

EIGHT SECONDS FROM HUMAN   89

How utterly degrading to be ruled by such base impulses, he thought. *For every one of the universe's secrets we uncover and add to the list, we are no better, no further removed, than the filthy rutting animals we truly are.*

Slaves to procreation and decrepitude.

The act of defecation was prolonged and relentless. Such was the richness that went down one end, such was the toxicity that went out the other. There was a lag before the air purifiers kicked in, so he was aware of the smell. The goddamn stink. The rot. The decay. Rushing out of him. The prospect of each blistering discharge a ticking timebomb.

How could something so vile have ever been inside him?

I hate what it is to be human.

He was encircled in a torrent of steam and sweat. Counting down the minutes, hoping against hope they would not mutate into hours. And so, he endured, until it was over.

Flush it all away.

Flushed all away into the emptiness of deep, deep space.

*

Later, ever the eye for things retro, he put on a replica NASA space suit. The suit was on the tight side, pinching in places, but such an irritant was worth it. It was worth the look.

The one exception to the retro feel were his gloves, which were state of the art, covered in tiny nodules, offering a heightened spatial awareness to the touch. Tucked under his left arm, he carried his space helmet.

A drone, *host droid* class, floated in attendance. It came with the ship.

The drone, magnetronic field fully operational, as depicted by a light blue hue, referred to Magnus's suit. 'Nice suit but you think it is a little too period

'Would you not prefer something more this century'

The drone, not wishing to cause offence, glowed a pale yellow. 'A suit with magnetronic shield capability at least'

Its field allowed it to manipulate objects. It also came with filters enabling it to change colour, which was intended to show character; a demonstration of underlying emotions. Some passengers, or guests as they were more commonly referred to, found this additional feature helpful, making it easier to bond with the machine over the duration of the journey.

For the most part, Magnus considered the droid's presence as frivolous. That part of the package he could do without. And he considered the droid's recent interjection as case in point.

Something more century. I'll show it something more century. Will a kick up the back chassis be more century enough for it? Trade it for scrap when I'm finished with it.

By way of reply, steely-eyed, Magnus held out the helmet in both hands to better examine it. The reflection of his face on the gold plating of the helmet's visor nodded its approval back at him.

"No, I would not." His voice was hoarse, but he rather liked the sound of it. Was in no mood to cough and clear his throat. "Do you know how hard I had to work to earn this downtime?"

At this, the drone could have provided the required computational analysis. It could have quantified the amount of energy expended by Magnus, accurate to the nearest kilojoule. But instead, it compressed its manipulator field in such a way it caused the air around it to flicker. The recycled azure air. And in so doing, it kept its own counsel.

"They call it R&R for a reason," said Magnus, in snoopy cap and audio headset. He flicked a fingernail on the visor of the helmet, making a *tnk-tnk* sound he also approved of. He took it to be reassuring. "Think of me as an alchemist, and I turn shit to gold."

Everything on the ship except Magus was an extension of Altair. The ship could exist outside of Magnus, but presently, vice versa couldn't be the case. They were joined at the hip. Shared a common purpose to be at a certain place at a certain time. It was just that their reasons for being there were very different.

"I'll wear what I damn well like," he chuntered.

There was silence. Magnus brought his helmet tight into his chest and closed his eyes and emptied his mind of all negative thoughts. He thought of waves hitting against a sea wall, his mind following the intricacies of every curl and twist of water. How the waves would disperse and regroup.

He was interrupted by a metal-on-metal speech pattern. 'Entering planetary orbit'

Altair's engines revved and rockets flared as it entered the orbit of a planet with a red glow.

'Below is the planet Bartholomew a Z-class planet'

The ship coasted along the planet's surface, adjusting height and speed where required. The ground underneath was a concrete jungle, showing signs of cracking and flaking. All of this interspersed by dead trees and deep-set erosion. Something happened here a long time ago; a cataclysmic event, a dismantling of civilisation.

'All higher life forms long declared extinct

'However recently there are developments'

There was movement below, a scurrying, so disturbed, brought about by changes in air pressure due to the presence of the ship. Out came an extended family of mutated humanoids. Showing ridged foreheads and compacted faces; short and stick thin. The bones in their bodies were shaped differently and pushed against their skin. All but withered away, but somehow still there.

'Recently,' the hollow voice continued to emanate around the ship—it was the ship— 'long range monitors have discovered pockets of activity of a primate humanoid nature warped and mutated and able to survive the ravages of an accursed earth'

Below, the indigenous population came to a stop as a group, crouching behind a crumbling concrete wall.

'I should clarify of a primate humanoid nature still pending'

Magnus stood, conscious he was stooping, with nil motivation to correct this.

"The Devolved," he said.

The host drone buzzed around him, glowing a ruby red. 'Please Magnus in civilised society the use of such terminology is considered the height of impoliteness'

Magnus put on his helmet, clicking it in place. He was, as they said back in the 21st Century, *suited and booted*.

"What do I care," he said. "I've been promised a hunt—and I earned this hunt—and a hunt Is what I'm going to have."

Landing gear in place, making its descent in near-vertical fashion, the ship resembled a giant short-limbed frog. It whipped up a dust storm of dirt and chipped concrete. And then it all came to a stop, and an eerie calm of before was restored.

A cabin door slid open soundlessly. Spaceman and drone walked and floated out respectively into the rays of a damaged oleaginous orange sky. Balanced in both Magnus's hands, still keeping to the retro theme, was a hunting las-rifle. And with that, they headed towards the crumbling wall.

Head angled, so he wasn't staring directly at the plasma star holding court in a cloudless sky, he said, "Too many."

'What number do you have in mind'

In response, Magnus raised one finger.

'Do you have a preference'

"Nope."

There was an air of impatience around Magnus. "Still nope."

Every one of the drone's receptors would have had to be inoperative not to pick up on this.

There was a click in the air, barely perceptible in audible terms but all the more deadly for it. The ship fired a missile, which separated in mid-flight into several smaller projectiles.

With a finger, Magnus had rid this planet of the notion of safety. He had dismantled the concept of shelter. Like a hot knife on one side. Butter on the other. The missiles both punctured the wall and despatched the group of humanoids in a flurry of crimson. Only one from the group was spared: an adult male, who stood in shock, his world torn asunder around it.

The humanoid stood exposed to the world. If it wasn't clear to it previously, it would be now, that it was the hunted.

Magnus shortened the length of his stride. He held his rifle at a diagonal tight on his chest. Everything within his control had so far gone to blah-blahdy-blah. Everything except one thing.

The humanoid, its pupils fully dilated, began to moan softly with no prospect of cessation. Its every sinew straining without moving at all.

"Make it run," Magnus said.

Such a task was best suited for the drone. Appearance-wise, it was a tiny replica of the mother ship. Even while acknowledging this, Magnus fought the inclination to think of it as baby Altair.

A panel slid open from the drone's main chassis and the barrel of a cannon appeared. It could fire numerous projectiles and beams of various threat levels. It selected rapid fire and there followed a series of small explosions chopping up the ground around the humanoid's feet. Reintroducing the imperative of fight or flee back to proceedings. The humanoid chose the latter.

"Better," Magnus commented.

Not lost to the outside world. The outside worlds. The drone had all frequencies open.

'According to the live feed' its voice modulation crackled, 'taking place on an adjacent belt currently in session the senate representing this vector is debating whether the indigenous population of the planet Bartholomew should be awarded human status

'Such as the one we are presently hunting'

Hearing the news, Magnus shook his head warily. "I can just see it. Such a grand domelike structure with members in robes dealing in long-winded platitudes, they push the debate on. All those diplomatic drones buzzing around, tripping over themselves, if they had any feet, to do their masters' bidding. Never deviating below shoulder height because that would be considered somehow disrespectful. Taking place even when there is zilch to discuss. Absolutely hee-haw to talk about."

'That may be so' the drone said in its default neutral voice, 'but the Solar Lady Marmaughton of the Third Een currently speaks for the Proposition'

'A vote will be called for soon enough'

The humanoid continued to run, cautiously, to

guard against its feet catching any of the sharp shards formed on the surface. It ran through a copse of dead trees believing that these would provide it with sufficient cover. Softer ground lay tantalisingly ahead.

Magnus kneeled and aimed his rifle. Now the preamble was taken care of, he was happy to take over. He trusted his mind and instincts; these were the things that had got him here after all. This was his reward for designing a penal facility that observed the seven facets of infinite compassion, including the tricky, often elusive aspect of blissful happiness. Mind and instincts—and the sights of his rifle, which provide an optic prompt, a design feature selected by him, ensuring perfect aim.

He squeezed the trigger and a smart bullet eviscerated a tree. Another squeeze, another tree rendered into disassociate particles. Dead trees made somehow deader.

The humanoid ducked at the sound of the first tree's destruction, flinched at the second, and was no longer afforded the luxury as the whine of the third bullet rang through the air and found its target.

Right leg hit, taking away what was below the knee. The world had shifted away. All that was left was the residue of momentum, causing it to fall and scrape along the jagged surface, with handfuls of dust its only respite.

Time now for Magnus to be back on his feet. His mind drifted to the journey awaiting him back home. What did they say? *Home is where the heart is.*

He'd left it there for safe keeping.

"Best not to dilly-dally."

On the approach, his thoughts took on a darker but familiar turn.

How utterly degrading to be ruled by such base impulses.

The humanoid was down on its side, head obscured, having assumed the foetal position. The slenderest of trails was all that remained of the bottom half of its leg. It was silent, not breathing. It was still.

Slaves to procreation and decrepitude.

Magnus was several feet away, rifle butt held hard against the shoulder. This close in he could void the weapon's optics and still be certain of the shot.

'Magnus'

Magnus held a hand up in the drone's direction. Time for everything to stop.

"Give me space," he said.

The drone acquiesced, emanating puce while keeping its distance.

There was another shift. The humanoid was elevated suddenly from the waist up, twisting around at the hips. It had a clump of concrete in its hand, which it threw with all its might in its tormentor's direction.

That same split second, Magnus had already responded by firing a bullet which ripped a hole in the humanoid's shoulder.

There was a thud…

The concrete smashed into the helmet visor, reduced on impact to little more than a cloud of dust. Following the thudding sound, there was a *tnk-tnk*.

There was a second.

From the drone, the equivalent of a metal shriek, joined by the darkest shade of red. 'No no no no'

Now the dust had settled, both spaceman and drone could see a concrete shard embedded in the visor. Tiny cracks had appeared, moving in ragged diagonals on either side.

"It's fine," Magnus said.

'I would not say so

'You are compromised your suit is not fit for purpose you need to return to the ship immediately'

The humanoid was on his back. Its latest injury had taken more out of it than a shoulder. The limbs that remained now even more broken and irregular. The only sign of life was that the low moan had returned, borne of the realisation of what it had lost. And of the limited time it had left. Still, there was time to mourn.

Magnus had no way of knowing any of this. Not that he cared. He looked down at his prey and felt invincible. No longer tethered to the world by the limits of physicality. An alchemist turning lead into gold. He could rise above it all. The sole arbitrator of life and death, but life was not a choice. Not one that he at all recognised.

Nothing could happen to him, not when he felt like this. Godlike.

Magnus turned towards the floating drone. "Make that the only update you have for me."

The drone host drifted on the threadbare daylight. Its AI mind both conscious of the fact it did not belong here but also that this place may have need for it very soon.

'Room for one more surely' it said.

'Matters in the Senate have become rather heated

'Members of the ultra-humanist faction *The Moral Border* have stormed the debating chamber

'Oh my resulting in fisticuffs

'There appears to be no resolution in sight'

Harnessing the contradiction of wanting to savour the experience and get it over with, such an effortlessly human condition, the hunter returned to the hunted. "You hear that? The Senate can't decide whether to call you and your kind human. Raise this shitty planet above a pitiful Class Z. You'd have every protection. Although some would argue human rights shouldn't be that easy to come by. They seem to be fighting over it right now."

The makings of a smile crept across his face. "Fighting over *you*."

He crouched and rested his rifle on the ground. "Me, personally, either way, I don't care. I have my R&R. If I'm not here, I'm in some other godforsaken part of the quadrant."

He returned to a vertical position, standing over the humanoid. He placed his boot on its neck, nudging the toe box in, so he had clear access to the throat.

"Perhaps we could help enlighten you?" Magnus continued. "Take you on a crash course. Less rock throwing and more, you know, sharing a bottle of your favourite red at a little mezzanine restaurant in a coastal town. Or how to light up a room where the only things in your possession are dazzling wit and twirling bowtie.

"Maybe chew the fat."

The humanoid was silent now, body fading. But it opened his eyes. It stared up at the gold-plated visor poised over him. This ferocious, unwanted stranger, but at least it had left its mark.

The cracks on the helmet were larger now. Creating spirals. A red light blinked on and off on one glove.

"But I'm here now, so let's make the best of it." Magnus, boot in position, began to exert pressure, down on the humanoid's throat.

Meanwhile, at Magnus's side, the drone turned a metal green. 'Order in the Senate has been restored a snap vote is taking place

'Vote is on a knife edge it could go either way'

Magnus adjusted his weight, applying more pressure. There was a deafening crack, which seemed too loud, too abrasive, to be anything other than the product of his imagination.

The humanoid's frame could only shudder.

Make it move.

'We are expecting the result in seconds

'Eight to be exact'

Puppet on a string.

'Eight Seven Six'

The drone was recalibrating. The protocol to protect everything human was imprinted on all AI. If the vote came in favour of the indigenous population, and there were still life signals to speak of detected from the fallen humanoid and Magnus demonstrated no attempt to back away, it would have no choice but to incapacitate its guest. As an anticipatory measure, it charged up its cannon.

For Magnus, the outcome did not matter. It was irrelevant. He was half aware that the drone's attention had now shifted to him; its magnetronic field having changed to ruby red.

He was aware that the air had emptied from his lungs. There was only the air of Bartholomew, too thin for a *human* to breathe.

But still, he willed himself on.

'Five Four'

There was the possibility of a reaction. Broken daylight broke some more.

The rifle in touching distance on the ground.

'Three Two'

And who to save in so little time.

Bodily functions shutting down.

'One'

He hated what it was to be human.

MANCHESTER

Rays of light streamed out of a circular hole in the sky and Andrew was left wondering how the world will end.

He was seated in his living room with a cold cup of hot chocolate cradled in his hands. His fingernails were filthy and his clothes frayed. He was unshaven, dishevelled, had not been sleeping well. He was deep in thought and not a little pissed off. He sported a quiff like a two-bit Elvis or a discounted Morrissey.

Will it be quick? he thought. *Will I die alone and in Manchester?*

He slurped at his hot chocolate. Such was the cold-ness of the water, the cocoa powder hadn't fully dis-solved, giving the drink a wholly gritty taste.

The grit took him back to the best part of two weeks ago. It was a different world at that point. So different even his most recent memories of that time now seemed unfamiliar to him.

The best part: facing him was his estranged wife Fiona, her mouth forming forceful words in the attempt to shake him out of his reverie. She tried to speak to him, but the truth was it had been a long time since he could engage with her in any meaning-ful manner. You didn't need an extinction event to reveal that particular home truth.

Anyway, it proved a quick conversation. Mercifully

so for all involved. It ended with Fiona and their two daughters—one nine, the other eleven—having hurriedly packed, rushing out to the car parked in the drive. She was taking the kids and she was intending to join the countrywide pilgrimage out of the cities.

He let them go. He chose to stay. No hard feelings either way.

No interest in leaving the house, even after the power was switched off. There was no heat and there wasn't much fat on his bones, but even so, he didn't feel the cold either.

His life wasn't that great before the crisis. He'd lost his job at the backend of last year and his response was to mope around the house and question what he was doing with his life, while doing nothing with his life. When she was around, Fiona wanted him to speak to someone, but he didn't know what he could possibly say. When there was blatantly nothing to him. When he was hollow inside.

Now he was alone, he believed he was being watched. Monitored by someone outside his line of vision but could sense they were there anyway. He did not think the watcher had malevolent intentions. They were there to record events and he was there to be recorded. Perhaps he just needed company; not friends or family, but someone he could relate to. And he hoped in a noncommittal way that the watcher might turn out to be one such person.

He stood at the curtains, peering out from his living room. The world was about to expire, and all scientific supposition supported this. But as he looked out on the tiny piece of Manchester that was his street, everything seemed quiet.

Reports up until two days ago (when the power had stopped) screamed otherwise. In Manchester itself, Beetham Tower was brought down by an electrical storm. London suburbs are plagued by sunbursts. A cyclone wiped out Rotherham.

A palpable feeling of oppression had descended, which made life intolerable.

A screaming pressure would build and rage inside his skull, it would get to the point he'd resemble the famous Munch painting.

In Cardiff and other cities, outbreaks of a psychotic nature. Public stoning, self-immolation, neighbour-on-neighbour cannibalism. Corpses that would normally litter the streets were gathered up and nailed on walls in the sign of a cross. The old religions were never far away.

Andrew remembered vividly the evening when the Prime Minister made his last public address. Every last detail, which was broadcast on a loop, and got to the point it was all you could watch for a fortnight. He thought of it often. There was a patina of sweat to be found on the PM's brow. You could not see where one droplet began and one ended. It gave his forehead a glossy finish.

"The pilgrimage is now national policy," the PM said while fighting a cough. "His Majesty's Government and I believe that the countryside, away from built-in areas, provides protection from the bio-electrical forces at large that are ravaging our cities.

"I repeat to be clear, move away from built-in areas."

The PM stopped to take a sip of water. Once done, the glass stayed in position, held in his hand at a slight angle, the surface still engaged with his bottom lip. The glass became a proxy, an umbilical cord, and it seemed an eternity before he finally succumbed and placed it back down on the table next to him.

"The police and armed forces will personally guarantee your safety," he continued, unsteadily, swallowing down hard, a moment of panic in his eyes as he looked down, again, at his glass. "People of the UK, take advantage of the seasonally benign weather for January and head to the country."

It was all a lie. A lie in terms of being an obvious falsehood, borne of good intentions maybe, a show of false bravado, designed to give false hope. Perhaps seeking to invoke some idealised view locked inside the Great British psyche, invoking children escaping the blitz of World War II and seeking refuge in the countryside. Andrew had no proof to back this up, just some thoughts and some deeply held suspicions. He had never voted for the PM and had never much liked the countryside. Such thoughts came to him when he first saw the broadcast three weeks ago, and he held the same mindset currently.

Outside, it was quiet. A pure silence that began to loom and take on a preternatural presence, and for the first time in a long time, Andrew felt truly alone. Maybe, he reasoned, he should take advantage of the quiet as in the calm before the storm. And after. It was time to break out of his self-imposed exile and engage once more with the world.

Up to this point, he was dishevelled, unshaven, his hair an untidy explosion, an appropriately glum demeanour attached to his face. He took a shower—cold, of course, the water little more than a trickle—but never wavering, he was set on his chosen course. He shaved and wore his most smart but casual clothes. He put a comb through his hair, which brought much-needed order to the unruly quiff. He even considered cutting his nails. He tested out a few expressions on the mirror and selected the one he considered closest to something like positive thinking. A transformation of sorts.

He picked up his mobile, having laid dormant like him for several days. Before this, he'd gone through the phase of checking his phone every five minutes for a message from his family. There was none, triggering bouts of acrimony, flashes of anger, of uncharacteristic spite, culminating in the decision to save what sanity he had left and switch the thing off entirely. But as he did so, he noticed the red bar at the top of the screen. He would charge it later, he decided, when his mood lightened. Only by then, there was no power and the decision was taken out of his hands.

And now, he looked down at his phone, still switched off, almost completely useless to him, but with a tiny charge, a glimmer of life residing inside it. He rested it on the palm of his hand and he felt strangely secure. It was there; it wasn't a figment of his imagination. He could put it away in his back pocket; save it for some time later. There was a warmth inside, ridding him of the feeling that someone was watching him.

If he was to make any real use of the phone, he would squeeze what little sense of life and momentum out of it he could; he would use it as motivation to spur him on. He walked out of the house. He walked into the deserted, embattled streets. There was an empty feeling all around and in the pit of his stomach. The weight of the air now took the place of everyone that had left. Nature abhorred a vacuum.

He stared up at the sky, which was clear except for two prominently placed clouds. A ray of light broke through, heading straight for him. Intuitively he held his hand out and the light bounced off his open palm. He squealed with delight at the spectacle. It seemed such an unnatural reaction, out of step with his current situation, and yet there they were: butterflies in his stomach. He gravitated with a skip towards the city centre.

He ploughed on. The air was balmy and sticky when it should not have been.

The seasons had been turned on their heads. The shrubbery was overgrown. Piccadilly Gardens was overrun. Broken tramlines. The roots of trees broke out of the tarmacked road and wrapped themselves around post boxes. Pollen accumulated and danced in the air like clouds of insects.

On Portland Street, he encountered three abandoned cars arranged in a triangle. Through the gap between the vehicles, he saw something unexpected which called for a double take.

Yes, it was unmistakable. In the middle of this metal triumvirate, the shape of another human being, lying on her back. She had short hair, dressed in a t-shirt and ankle-length skirt. Her arms at rest on either side, eyes closed, a demeanour akin to someone sunbathing.

A shadow fell on her.

She opened her eyes. Alert, she uncoiled and sprung to her feet. There was a rock in her hand.

"Who are you?" Andrew asked. Or tried to. Just about finishing the words when a wide swipe of the rock struck his temple.

Andrew dropped down to one knee, his head spinning, his brow leaking a trickle of blood. It took him an elasticated moment to claw back his bearings.

"Wait," he said. "I'm sorry."

She stooped and grabbed his arm. "Who are *you*?" she said.

Andrew couldn't adequately react or enunciate the words. He just looked at her with lost puppy eyes, forcing her into a further response of her own. She raised her hand and placed it on his cheek, her fingertips dabbed the blood that congealed there.

"Are you real?" she asked.

"It's tomorrow…" he said at last. "World's going to end tomorrow."

*

Her name was Moira, and she was taller than Andrew. She could effortlessly hold his gaze for several seconds. Unless there was a good reason for it, she found it impossible to be still. She pinched an earlobe when she was nervous.

Earlier, she had tended to his wound, which immediately began to scab over. That night, they stayed at a room in the Hotel Gotham. They picked the biggest room, which was the honeymoon suite. If the irony of this was not lost on them, the violence of their first meeting still fresh in their minds, neither of them showed it.

They shared a cavernous bed and, both exhausted, bodies aching and cramping, fell instantaneously asleep. They slept without dream.

When they awoke, they cuddled and revelled in the warmth of another human being. They talked of their fears and hopes, and how utterly meaningful and pointless a conversation such as this was. All at the same time.

"Can we forgive each other?" he said.

"There's nothing to forgive," she said.

"Please."

"Sure, then, I forgive you everything, always and forever."

They rose for breakfast. While one of them kept watch for dogs and rats, having claimed much of the city now that the humans had left, the other scavenged for food in the kitchens. They found a pack of dried rolls, surprisingly not too far past their sell-by date.

They relocated to the dining area, which was ornate and spacious, and sat at a round table and began to eat. Andrew couldn't take his eyes off her, took delight at every tiny, considerate bite, like she had all the time in the world. If he thought about it, perhaps he'd regret taking so long to venture out into the world in the first place. Embarking on those first tentative steps on the garden path, the thud of the front door swinging shut behind him. The conscious undertaking of a hop and a skip still days away. But for now, watching someone eat, another thing in a past life they'd taken for granted and then thought they'd never see again, he wouldn't change a thing. It was perfect.

The dried roll was unremittingly dry and flaky.

"Is dying of thirst on the itinerary?"

"Nope, I believe we can park that for next time."

"Best find a flushed toilet before we leave."

"This is the life."

Before they left, they wanted to sign the hotel guest book, but they couldn't find a pen for the life of them. So, they stood at the exit and bellowed out their review.

"Sheets hadn't been changed for weeks. I won't be back!"

"This hotel gave me dysentery. I will be back!"

Outside, they walked side by side in the direction of an electrical storm.

Not far from them, the Town Hall in Albert Square was hit and decimated by lightning. The building, the clock tower without and the offices and ceremonial rooms within, gave little resistance as if it realised its time was up, collapsing like a matchstick display.

"Need a minute," Andrew said. He knew in his gut that this was the time—this was the moment—and he wouldn't have another chance. He switched on his phone.

The phone screen lit up. It was literal white light. The light seeped out of the casing and formed a corona around the device. He peered down and sensed that at least part of him could plunge into the light. In return, this would give him insight into so many things.

He would not hesitate to venture forth and expand his horizons this time. He dived in. Miles from here, towards the countryside, there was a traffic jam on a motorway, stretching as far as the mind could see. In a synaptic flash, the neural equivalent of a blink of an eye, he jumped to the end of the gridlock to find the cause. It was a military checkpoint.

The checkpoint was deserted, except for a soldier in his twenties. In shock, pupils like saucers, holding up a rifle, tensed, poised to fire, words of desperation dressed as warning come tumbling out. "Halt or I'll—"

A woman, out of her wits to the point of feral, on all fours, thumped into him, knocking him to the ground. Ensnared in the melee, the soldier fired harmlessly past her. The woman responded in kind by biting into his throat.

Close by, emboldened, made wild by the scent of blood, a gang with metal fused in their skin attacked a car. The leader, howling, veins prominent in neck and forehead, punched through the front passenger side window. While other gang members kicked and shook the car. The occupants were screaming, understandably so.

Andrew checked himself. He censored the mind. He didn't want to go further. Didn't want to see who was inside.

His mind now shifted to the dark. Immovable and intransigent. A dark that could never be light. There were shadows on shapes and shapes on shadows that indicated wherever this was it was outside. And it was exposed.

He was in the countryside. His focus was on a teenager, bald, hunched, and dressed in rags. His tattooed face was a muddle of Mayan hieroglyphics, signifying a Mesoamerican civilisation that foretold the end of the world. Some light reasserted itself as evidenced by the torch he held in his hand. You could make out his face, contorted with undiluted hatred.

The teenager was not alone, joined by a mob, boys and girls, each bald and misshapen, with Mayan tattoos and torn clothing. They shined their torches at a grown man crouching down, frightened, his back up against a tree, clutching a baby close to him. Several members of the mob reached out towards him, whispering of the old gods, intent on bloodletting and sacrifice.

Meaning to snatch the baby.

Flashes of torchlight illuminated the father's terrified face. Likewise, the faces of the mob came into view; aged as young as nine or eleven.

Andrew recoiled. His mind fled from the insanity. From the savagery and barbarism. And from more besides.

It hadn't taken long, the descent. So, that was the countryside.

A pile of dead bodies. Limbs entwined; wounds congealed; conjoined corpses. A totem to extinction. He could see the faces if he wanted to. It was in his phone's gift. He could check if his family was there.

He was sure that he missed them. And it had been so long since he'd last seen them now that time has stretched into nothingness. But from what he'd seen, peering in, he was certain no good would come of it…

No. Again, he withdrew and went back. Didn't want anything to ruin his perfect day.

Mercifully, the phone went dead and Andrew, body and mind, was back in Manchester. He was so much more aware. On one side was Moira. On the other, he could see more of the light from the corner of his eye. This time emanating from a metal machine, floating, static, a drone of some kind. A technology not belonging to this world.

Up until this point, there was a filter in place to shield the drone from view. But the light—he had grown so sensitive to it—had grown so intense it could no longer remain hidden. What appeared to be Mayan hieroglyphics adorned its plating.

It was self-aware, evolving, as advanced a piece of recording equipment as this corner of the universe could allow. It was all relative of course. Relative to this part of the universe, but what could not be denied was the Stellarbyte of memory the drone had at its disposal. Virtually unlimited. A well that never runs dry.

The light ignited his mind again, and Andrew could see the cosmos laid out in front of him. Only a glimpse, mind you, the sheer scale of it beyond him. He was aware of the map the drone took to journey here, tapping into the nuclear fusion generated by a hundred suns along the way.

This was its latest assignment. This was coming to an end. The machine preparing to refuel on the latest solar flare to dominate the skyline. As it readied to leave this world for home.

He sensed no malevolence from the machine. It was here to take notes and learn. If only to confirm that no matter how great the civilisation that all things must come to an end. Even in Manchester.

For Andrew, the important aspect was that it was documenting events. It was documenting him—them—it.

Less important was the confirmation this brought; that he was being watched all along. It was watching everything. The drone was recording the end of the world.

He felt love for the machine. And for its home world wherever and whatever this was. He felt love for everything around him. And then, there was a sensation, a feeling of rotation, head pounding, stomach churning. And then, it was gone.

"Did you see it?" he said.

"I saw it all," she said.

"You ready?"

"Of course."

Moira and Andrew were blinded by a sunburst that filled the sky. It filled the world. They had no idea if the effects would be temporary, but this would hardly seem to matter now. The light was inside them, flowing out of their fingertips, streaming out of their eyes.

He reached out towards her and found and took her hand. They could hear the thunder booming around them and were happy to anticipate the lightning that would surely follow.

Holding both hands now, Moira and Andrew adjusted their stance so they faced each other. Andrew was smiling and he was certain she was smiling too. He leaned forward towards her and she reciprocated in kind.

Searing heat enveloped them, the thermal energy which followed threatening to lift them off their feet. The environment around them no longer solely external, it was inside them too, boiling their blood, vaporising what remained of their humanity from the inside out.

Will it be quick? he'd wondered. *Will I die alone and in Manchester?*

It would have to be yes to all of these, he reckoned. That is, except for one.

WHEN WILL I BE FAMOUS

When will I be famous?

Trust me, this isn't as odd or as contrived a question from a complete nobody as you might think. At least in my humble opinion. Once you spend some time with me, get a glimpse of the genius I carry around me like a reversible backpack, I have this suspicion it won't be long before you're asking the very same thing.

Let's not duck around the bush, shall we. Now, what kind of fame am I after? I don't want to be ultra-famous, you know, like George Clooney, or George Clooney's wife. I just want the type of respect and love that excuses those moments in public when you find yourself sweating profusely, or experiencing trapped wind (in my experience one usually follows the other). A world where the people, the world press, carpet dwellers of social media everywhere, will explain away such incidents as showing character; the demonstration of a raging mind and a burgeoning febrile spirit. What I don't want everywhere I go is adoring fans throwing petal-shaped soft-centred chocolates at my feet. Nothing so gaudy or over the top or potentially messy, what with me having two left feet. No sirree. No thanks.

I'm not an unreasonable man. If I come across as brusque, as rude even, it's because I'm too busy being myself to worry about all the airs and graces.

What do I do? I write visionary sci-fi. Visionary because I'm in my forties and still unpublished. Well, that's not technically true as I've had plenty of offers to publish my various works and in return hand over thousands of pounds for the pleasure. And I don't blame them. If they were responsible for unleashing my genius on an unsuspecting public then they'd be equally culpable for the many established authors exposed to my prescient text and bottomless talent and ideas without boundaries who, as a consequence, would be reduced to tears and not much else. Faced with coming to terms with the error of their ways with no option open to them other than to step down and desist from writing immediately. They'd need to set up a compensation fund for them.

So far, alas, I've not been able to convince the government to loan me the cash to finance my publishing ventures, though there are plenty to choose from. I've sent letters to everyone I can think of: the (not really in my opinion) great and the (ditto) good, addressing my many letters to 'My Local MP – whoever you are' and 'King Eddie/Charlie/Willy III/IV/V – delete where appropriate.'

My conviction remains strong despite all the detractors. The unbelievers, as I like to call them. I pop copies in the post of the first five pages (triple-spaced, naturally) of my latest unsolicited magnum opus to every publisher and agent listed in the *Writers and Artists Yearbook* from 1988. Yes, 1988. I ask my local library at least seven times a week to order in a more recent edition. I beseech them, anything from the last thirty years will do!

So, in my latest story called *Pursuit of Perfection*, where a private detective called Arthur Paradigm, body bedazzled with various machine parts, is considering what addendum to buy next. At the same time, he is constantly called away to attend a protracted hostage negotiation involving mutant bunnies and warrior nuns. Sometimes it's the bunnies taking the nuns hostage, sometimes it's the other way around.

The burning question at the centre of *PoP* is this: at what point does Paradigm, with all his robotic augmentations, lose his humanity? Also, can he save the hostages? Plus, throw in a love triangle involving him, a fanatical buck and a kickass nun. Without wanting to put words into peoples' mouths, it's a genre classic in the making.

I'm still waiting for the vast majority to reply, more fool them. Of the responses I did get, many consisted of a scribbled note that reads *no forwarding address.* But others were more specific, but no less hurtful, no less misguided. *Thank you for your submission. Unfortunately, it reads like a first draft with no obvious regard for grammar or spelling, or even the correct understanding of words. Can I suggest you invest in a dictionary? And perhaps a thesaurus?*

And that was one of the better ones. Other cuts of the deep variety include:

Horrible and absurd.

Ideas, if you can call them that, that are all over the place.

No merit whatsoever.

Do you know where the publisher you're writing to has gone because he owes me money?

I grieve for the tree that died so this abomination could be committed to paper.

A dog's mess.

A kangaroo's mess.

Laughable, tragic, hysterical – but not in a good way.

Never contact me again!

I have a suspicion that you still live with your mother.

I live with my mother? My *mother*?! What a suggestion! How dare they? How could they postulate such a thing? I'm about to start stamping my feet in protest when there is a knock at the door.

"Hullo," a shrill, nervous voice imparts from the other side of the door. "I have a cup of tea and one of those nice biscuits you like. You're not playing with your doodah, are you?"

My dear old mum once walked in on me when I was in the act of alleviating my tortured psyche. The shock of it all caused Mater to throw the mug she was carrying in the air. The resulting explosion of mild to hot liquid exacting a first-degree burn around her thumb area, not to mention the fatal cracking of my favourite Luke Skywalker mug. All told, an unfortunate incident. It's for the best that she knocks first.

"Enter, Mother," I say in my deepest, dark-side-styled voice.

I feel a little better after several gulps of sweet tea and the consumption of a chocolate bourbon (one is rarely enough and I might go searching later in the biscuit tin for another).

But it's not long before my thoughts return to the barbed comments from those who should know better. Why so cruel? Wasn't this in actuality one human being reaching out to another and baring their soul? Seeking words of kindness and gentle encouragement. Not nihilism.

I cannot sleep. I scratch my skin to the point I draw blood. Why can't they see? I have a voice, a true voice, why don't they hear? We are talking about nihilism of the worse kind. What are they afraid of?

I have no choice but to go on. To go out. I meet up with my good friend Alistair at a pub just outside Queen Street station. We refer to it as *The Casket*. That's not its real name, but that's what we call it. The pub is a favourite establishment of Alistair's because it sells fortified wine. At the bar, he orders an MD 20/ 20 Blue Raspberry for himself and a half pint of Tennent's for me.

"MD for me," Alistair says as he sits at our table. "MD for the Mad Dog at the table."

He takes a middling to large slurp of the azure blue

liquid. "Ah, 2020," he adds. "Now that was a good year."

He says this a lot. Every time he settles down to a MD, in fact. I have no good reason, bar a nagging persistent feeling that alternates between my gut and the back of my head, to suggest MD doesn't stand for Mad Dog. However, it feels like I'm on surer ground thinking 20/20 doesn't represent the year it was brewed. There's no MD 20/19 or MD 20/21, or MD 18/97 for that matter. I am pretty sure this is Alistair's idea of a joke.

"How goes your latest magnum opus?" he asks.

"WIP," I answer.

"WIP it is," he says, his voice little more than a whisper, so I can't quite make out the tone to ascertain the nature of it. "C'mon," a little louder now, "let's be having you."

I wish I was sure his interest was genuine. That we were two like-minded souls who meet on the first Thursday of every month (except January), eager to share their respective nuggets of gold. But if Alistair has any nuggets, he keeps them close to his chest. Or more precisely, he reassures me all his stories are alive and well and safely stored inside his head. He assures me that also he has a massive brain. And if unleashed on an unsuspecting and undeserving (his words) public, they would push out the boundaries of science fiction and fantasy, etc, etc. He's got a Hugo Award locked in there. A Nebula Award. To borrow one of his favourite phrases: *It would blow their bloody minds.* I have to take his word for this because I've not heard or read anything to contradict him. To my knowledge, he has never committed anything to audio, or to paper, or on screen.

"Donkey Kong, you say?"

"No, the Mule King," I say as I relate the denouement of my latest work in progress. So, we have the Tactonians on one hand, the Ractonians on the other, and the Lizard Folk on a third hand, and to a Tactonian, Ractonian and lizard they are all after Ben Benfica because he is a— "

I use my fingertips to affect a drum roll on the table. "Drug mule in space. He has the drug Sasquatch Spice concealed in a kinder egg shoved up his very human back passage.

"But here's the twist. No one cares about the Sasquatch. Benfica's physiology is spliced with strands of earth mule DNA. And, as has been rigorously explained in the middle chapters previously—which I've still to write—hidden in his DNA is the key to unlocking the secrets of creation itself.

"All three alien races are long evolved from either alien horses or alien donkeys, but up to this point they can't mate with each other for fear of having mule offspring, and as we know mules are universally infertile. But Benfica has twenty-seven children and counting: Harry-1 all the way up to Harry-27. As a result, he's the most sought-after part-human/part-mule in the universe…"

"Thas a good shtory, lotsh of poshibilities." Alistair, now on his third Mad Dog, was slurring his words. "Not ash good ash the baby I have locked upsh here shafe and shound." He pointed shakily towards the middle of his forehead.

I checked my watch. "We've reached that time."

"Forty-five minutessh already? Mushn't be late."

A brisk five-minute walk later and we arrive at the Tron, venue of tonight's *Cat's Cradle* meeting. This is the writers' group of choice for local sci-fi visionaries everywhere, but mostly those within travelling distance of Glasgow.

We're fashionably ten minutes early. Well, fashionable for me and Alistair. No Mad Dog here, so I buy a pint of European lager for him and a half pint of European lager for me.

I pass a mic on a stand, perched on a dais, which lies dormant for the time being. I join Alistair at our usual corner and give him his drink. No hint of a thank you, but I've grown used to his ways. Others arrive and we shuffle our feet and cast the odd conspiratorial glance at no one in particular as the mingling around us begins.

All the wild trappings of self-promotion and flappy hands and jog-awful commentaries are in play here. *I'm meeting that someone; my agent told me this much; I'm up for an award for that thing; Netflix are interested in this and Apple TV+ that; a two-book deal; my publisher loves me; literally the best thing pound-for-pound I have ever written.*

"My round," Alistair says, inspecting his empty glass, having drained the contents in no time at all.

I still had two-thirds of my half pint remaining. "Nothing for me. Thanks."

Replenished pint in hand, Alistair does not return to our corner. Instead, he ingratiates himself with the other groups. Occasionally nodding his head in my direction, a clear indication he is talking about me. And you can tell by the sneer on his face that he's no longer slurring his voice, and that he is not being complimentary at all. The heat rises up from my collar and I begin to sweat profusely. I lift my beverage to my mouth, only to miss it entirely, but the liquid needs to go somewhere. A damp patch emerges on my chest.

Every time. Without fail. Call me a fool, a misguided optimist, but I always hope that this time he won't end up taking the piss. He won't use me as his way in with the in-crowd. Or any crowd. I'm always willing to give him the benefit of the doubt.

One of the organisers steps up to the mic and introduces the first speaker.

A writer I recognise as Rudolph Manchild (because that's his name) steps up to the dais. He wears a white jumper with black stripes, so resembling a bumpy zebra crossing. Everyone stands quietly. My chest remains sodden. If there is a celestial being out there, then I fancy this is the time to prove its existence and make the damp go away.

Manchild squares up to the mic, unfolds a single page of A4 paper, and takes a deep breath.

"Hail our new Overlords!" he bellows. "Imagine a world overrun by giant one-eyed insectoids…"

For the next three days I am mostly confined to barracks—or bed as it is more commonly known. I'm not depressed, but I'm down all right. But self-doubt is temporary while class is permanent, so with this in mind eventually I rise. I shake off the cobwebs and put the kettle on and go check my email.

It's the usual spam content. Everyone wants to be my wife or for me to inherit their fortune, but never both, funnily enough. No one wants to publish my work. I see I have a notification from Twitter.

Pride prevents me from following more people on Twitter than follow me, but lo and behold upon log in, I note I now have eight followers! The latest one to add to the ranks is @EdgarC73! And I have a message from that very same Twitterer, which reads like so:

My name is Edgar Comeuppance and I am a
big fan of your work! Please can we meet?
Give me a time and location at your earliest
convenience. Regards!

Up until this point I had never heard of a Comeuppance. Previously, I would have quite happily numbered him as one among the eight billion, nine billion (who has time to count?) souls around the planet to warrant my complete indifference. You see, I am fundamentally a rational creature, but one susceptible to the odd bout of emotion. And the emotion I now felt having read the message was instant, unfiltered anger.

Hot blood pumping through my veins, I reply:

Who are you and why are you torturing me?
Go find some other sap to torment and

ridicule and sneer donw to. What type of
cretin uses a signoff like Regards! anyway?

I realise after sending I should have spellchecked. And now I don't care. I should have added a 'snarling' emoji. But now I definitely don't care. Did I say I didn't care?

Instantaneously, a reply to my reply:

No, you misunderstand. I adored your story
The Insensate, the alien race that sacrifices
its sense of taste in order to cross time
and space. I beg of you I am a massive fan who
only wishes to eulogise your talent.

And then a second reply to my reply:

I do not understand why you are not as
famous as Margaret Atwood or Yevgeny
Zamyatin. More famous even.

I am rather stunned to read this. I am close to tears, but in a good way. I am a wordsmith by vocation and words are my only nourishment; my only currency. And of course, they do say flattery can get you almost anywhere. How else to answer:

See you at half one tomorrow at Spill the
Beans in Shawlands, Glasgow, UK, Europe, Earth,
the Solar System, the Milky Way

The response is a simple one, but it is the world to me:

See you there!

That night, I sleep well. There is a warm glow which envelopes my body. During the night I wake suddenly, only for words of platitudes to be softly whispered in my ear, and I settle back down again.

The next day, at the anointed time, I enter Spill the Beans with enough change in my pocket to buy a piccolo latte. As I make my purchase, I'm suddenly thrown into a mild state of panic, fearful they might have put the prices up since the last time I was here. My skin becomes prickly with sweat. Thankfully that's not the case. I take my prize to the closest empty table next to a window.

I take a small sip of my beverage, careful not to slurp and waste any of the balletically frothy, intimately bitter liquid. As it slips down my throat, it occurs to me that I have no idea what @EdgarC73 looks like. There was no mention of wearing a rose or balancing a plastic duck on your shoulder, or any of the other things strangers do to stand out from the crowd. And I can only assume he inhabits the same hemisphere as me. And I'm still not convinced that this might not be someone's idea of playing a trick on me. Obviously, if this is the case, then the joke is on them, because here I am, latte in hand, with a view outside—admittedly of traffic travelling too fast in an inbuilt area.

The door swings open and a man in a navy trench coat strides in. He is over six foot tall, has straight black hair, and recently shaved. Immediately he locks eyes on me and he waves both hands in my direction. I'm tempted to look left and right of me, but I have caffeine in my veins, so I aim a tiny movement of my fingers, like I'm tapping on an invisible but fragile keyboard, back at him.

My eyes begin to moisten, which makes him literally a blur as he walks to the table and sits himself down on the vacant chair facing me.

He turns his head with an arm in the air, clicking his fingers. "Garçon, Garçon," he says.

"I think you need to order at the counter," I chip in.

"Oh, excellent of course, allow me. Another latte, perhaps?"

One quick nod later, and my head is swimming before I even begin my second coffee. "Edgar?" I say.

"At your service."

I note his beverage of choice is a speciality tea, no doubt containing jasmine.

"Is your surname really Comeuppance?"

He smiles at me. It is the widest smile I have ever seen. "Yes," he says.

I am unsure if I should smile back, so instead there follows a period of twitchy silence. I'm gripped by the forces of indecision.

"*Wall of Bread*," he says suddenly, leaning forward.

"You don't mean…" I wrack my brain at that one. Undeniably, the name of a short tale I authored. I certainly sent it out to a million and one different people. Did I publish online somewhere? Did someone do so on my behalf? Without my consent? With my consent? Perhaps, maybe, possibly?

There is obviously something he needs to say, so I give him space. He wraps his hands around his glass tea cup, drawing out the warmth. He begins:

"It feels as if I read *Wall of Bread* yesterday. Well, I did reread it yesterday, but it was one full month ago when I read it first. One glorious month. We have our main character, Tom, who is introduced to us standing on waste ground. Now, this isn't any ordinary waste ground. This waste ground is circled off by a wall consisting of giant slices of white bread. Each slice is big and tall enough that Tom cannot see over it. We realise at this point that Tom lives inside a Wall of Bread.

"It is bleak here, boring and demoralising. But there is more. With a squelch, Tom sticks his head through one of the slices of bread and peers out to the other side into even more waste ground. But this is different. There is Masha, the life-sized Music Box Ballerina. She strikes a classic pose. The music starts with a click and she dances. As far as Tom is concerned, she dances for him, and she takes him out of an otherwise empty and meaningless existence. And Tom plays his part. He watches on enthralled.

"However, the bread, which is sentient and responsive, is aware of Tom's presence. It grows stale and hardens around his neck and he needs to use both hands to push his head out and escape its starchy embrace. Tom yells at the top of his voice, such is the fearsome effort required to secure his escape.

"His head is free, and he falls to the ground exhausted. He is alone again, there is no Masha. But he cannot risk another peek through the bread, not today.

"Later, he attempts to sleep on his own patch of waste ground. He tries to blot out the wall, which whispers to him. The wall taunts him in that dry wheat germ murmur of its. Just out of Tom's vision, the wall makes its preparations. It works on reinforcing its defences so the day will come when Tom will not be able to push his head through ever again.

"Tom awakes to the sound of construction coming from over the wall. He takes a deep breath and pokes his head through the doughy white slice in front of him. On the other side, Masha dances, but she is not alone.

"He spies the scaffolding. A group of engineers work on a giant toaster. A crane lowers a slice of bread into one of the toaster's trays. Tom wonders if he should be concerned.

"—The End—"

Finished, Edgar sits back. He holds his tea up to his nose and inhales some steam.

I am stunned by this. Overwhelmed. Overjoyed. A tear begins to form in my eye.

"That's exactly how I wrote it," I say, aware that my body is beginning to shake and there is nothing I can do to prevent it. "To the word."

Another smile, this one threatens to crack Edgar's face open. "That is so right. So perfect. This is exactly how I remember it word for word. Your story speaks to me. It tells me of beauty in isolation. Of impossible yearning. It is the essence of what it is to be human. All of your stories are like this and all I want to do is reach out and help you fulfil your potential. For you to become sweet sir. The visionary in everyone's eyes that you are to me."

"You get me." I swallow, not coffee this time. I bite my bottom lip. "You get me."

I agree to meet Edgar for more latte and more tea the next day. We discuss another of my stories. *Machine Man* is set in a world where a government-sponsored procedure enables people to become near-immortal cyborgs. But there is a cost as the process also extracts the human soul.

At the end of the meeting, Edgar stares into my eyes and it's like he's peering into *my* soul.

"What do you want?" he says.

"I want people to read my work," I reply, my tone a little too flat to be properly convincing.

"What do you really want?"

I agree to meet Edgar for additional latte and additional tea the next day. We discuss a different story. This, a metaphysical, psychological piece entitled *The Last Human*, where humanity is the scourge of the universe and is hunted down to the point of extinction. Martha Coeur de Lion is the eponymous last human, only to realise that this brings with it a new and astonishing birthright.

She is destined for something dramatic and cool.

She is a product of destiny.

She is destined for godhood.

Now the bounty hunters are no longer hunting a weak, isolated human being, but in fact a god.

Edgar waits patiently for me to finish. He smiles—he always smiles—and then asks, "What do you want?"

"For people to love my writing and listen to what I have to say."

"What do you really want?"

"What do I really want?"

I agree to meet Edgar the next day for the very best hot beverages Spill the Beans has to offer once more. I am bristling with ideas and energy. Vying most for my attention is one such idea I have a title for, *The Impossible Choice*. In order to survive, an earth colony is faced with having to choose between the cold harsh reality of extinction or becoming vampires. WIP. I haven't worked out how the story starts, so I stumble over the words.

Edgar brings his finger to his lips, paternally so. Edgar is the flame and I am a moth.

"What do you want?"

"I've already said."

"No, you have not, not really."

"I…I…"

The room spins around me and I have no way of controlling this. Prickles of heat bubble up on the back of my neck and forehead. There is something inside me I've kept down there, long constrained, now unleashed.

"All the naysayers…"

"Go on," he says.

"All the nit-pickers, the self-grandiose critics, those who would reject me with their cruel barbs…"

"Go on."

"The faceless ones with no time or kindness in their hearts; the vanity publishers only interested in the words' pound and pence; my so-called friend who ditches me at the earliest opportunity…"

Flecks of spittle accumulate on my bottom lip. Edgar's eyes give the effect of widening while retaining the same shape.

"I want to show them up! Every last mother-bothering one of them!"

"Yes?"

"I want to be so famous I can rub their noses in it. Or pay someone to do it for me."

"Yes?"

"I want my revenge."

I only realise after the fact that I've been waving a clenched fist in the air. But for now, I am breathless and I am spent. My shoulders visibly sag.

As for Edgar, he sits back on his chair almost like it's not there. The lapels of his coat flap in a non-existent breeze as if they've taken on a life of their own. His fingers play an imaginary piano concerto on the table. "And now my dear friend, you are ready."

The following evening, I venture into The Casket for my weekly meet-up with Alistair my fair-weather associate. Alistair is already at the bar, ordering an MD 20/20 Dragon Fruit and a half pint of Tennent's.

"MD for me," Alistair says as he joins me at our usual table. "MD for the Mad Dog in The Casket."

He takes a swig of the sunset orange-red beverage. "Ah, 2020," he adds. "Now that was a good year."

I put my half pint down. I'd get to that later. "You know what," I say, "20/20 actually stands for 20 ounces and 20% proof, which back in the day, when the drink was first introduced, was the bang you got for your original buck.

"Eh?"

"And while I'm on the subject, MD stands for Mogen David, the wine company that first brewed it."

In response, Alistair pulls a myriad of stretched-out faces. "Get you," he says, eventually.

"Get me," he says, pointing an index finger at his forehead. "Locked in here, I've got game changers, I've got masterpieces, it would blow their bloody minds." Revitalised by this, a sparkle returned to his eyes, he continues, "How goes Donkey Kong WIP?"

I lift my half pint and take a sip. I'm in no hurry to answer, even though reply I must.

"Something new this time around. I'm on the mic tonight, so you'll hear it along with the rest of them."

I am happy to sit in silence and enjoy this new side to Alistair, who has become decidedly sheepish in my company. Intermittently, he appears to have thought of something to say, then checks himself. Periodically, the tip of his tongue sticks out of his mouth as he moves it from side to side. He orders a second MD, and a third, but on this occasion there is no evidence of slurring.

We arrive at the Cat's Cradle meet-up our customary ten minutes early. It's not long before Alistair plays to type and slopes off, but that hardly matters now. I only have eyes for that which is elevated on the dais. Which is straight, slender and permanent. Once the sight of it would have left me dumbfounded. I would shy away from its presence; its power. Now it is a siren I cannot ignore.

"What do you really want?"

I am aware of arrival and movement and the flapping of hands around me, but it's all peripheral. They say time is relative and they are right. For me, right this moment, time hurtles by.

My time has come, I decide. I don't wait for any official announcement. I take the stage in a single bound.

I'm level with the mic, which seems happy to see me. It sways and dances, appears as a portal in front of me. A gateway to self-expression, self-realisation. Albeit a narrow one.

I will not shirk the challenge.

Beyond the mic, I peer into the splashes of darkness that obscure those watching on. The odd snicker and cough aside, I am met by stunned silence.

I take a moment to replay in my mind Edgar's departing words. *Be natural. Just tell the story as it comes. Use those wonderful words of yours. Do not stop for breath.*

I believe in you.

"I'd like to read to you this evening (no notes) a story of mine called *Scratch*."

I begin.

"A comet embellished with a bright light halo, it

travels through the cosmos. What more does one need as reminder? Space. It's a big backyard.

"Lying in wait—in the comet's trajectory—a spaceship goes about its business. The ship, *The Ortiz*, is sleek and retro in design. Well, retro for the 25th Century. The ship has wings and a crew of twenty.

"The Ortiz is dedicated to uncovering the secrets of the universe. Whoosh!

"Inside, Joe the cabin boy floats along a main corridor towards the cockpit. Joe has a big mass of curly hair which stands firm despite the lower gravity. He has a sixteen-year-old boyish and freckled face, exuding boyish and freckled enthusiasm.

"Joe floats past a couple of technicians in one of the cabins, door open. The first technician is called Ken, while the other is Tiff. Ken, goofing around, balances an electronic clipboard on the top of his head. Tiff is smiling, but as smiles go, it's more of an impatient, sympathetic smile. She doesn't have the time for this.

"Ken and Tiff. According to Joe, nothing less than good people. That's what he's thinking as he floats past.

"Joe has this strong sense that Ken will serve on The Ortiz for another couple of years before returning to Earth to run an ostrich farm. As for Tiff, on the back of the discovery of a new, epoch-making space element, which she'll name after her aunt's cat, she will tour the known universe. A quick kiss between them at an impromptu party called by the captain a week ago will never amount to anything.

"Even though his feet don't touch the ground, Joe

can feel activity throbbing from below. The focus of his attention is the keel of the ship, covered by a thick malleable carbyne coating. The coating both repels and attracts, and sifts through the space-swirl of rubble, dust and vapour. It is the various specimens, which gather there to be considered for analysis, that justify the mission.

"The plan is, as the comet passes, for the ship to swoop in close to the comet's coma where the ship will isolate and crystallise particles and fragments. Analysis will begin instantaneously.

"All the while, the comet, named *Hastings*, laden with ice and rock approaches. Chok-a-block with amino acids and life-building elements. Hurtling through space, considered a bad omen back in really ancient times, the comet is both creator and destroyer of life.

"Back inside the ship, Joe's mind strays to the cockpit where the captain and co-pilot sit at the controls. They are looking outside the cockpit window, catching the first glimpse, at least with their own eyes, of the approaching Hastings.

"Captain Briggs calls the shots. In truth, he is worthy of a bigger ship and a larger crew. If it wasn't for his problem with alcohol, that is. And everyone's favourite co-pilot, Smithy. The current mission will turn out to be his last tour of duty. He will go on to make his fortune in the terraforming industry.

"Scratch that.

"Joe remains floating, still located in the corridor, but he's no longer moving, remaining stationary. On his face, there is a sorrowful tight little smile that belies his tender years.

"The final computations on approach will be slightly off, and for that blame Captain Briggs. A barely noticeable shake of the hand. Tiny margins, resulting in a chunk of comet rock, roughly a tenth of the size of The Ortiz, to shortly and unexpectedly smash into the ship.

"The effect will be catastrophic. Boom! Engulfed by a great fireball. All are lost. All their hopes and fears and furtive little kisses. The secrets of the cosmos, for the time being, to remain undisclosed.

"This is no longer idle speculation. It is happening now. There is a terrible impact. A wrenching of screaming metal.

"Joe remains in a stationary position, his lips pursed and head lowered. Behind him, a fireball engulfs the corridor.

"Creation. It's a big toolbox. And Joe should know."

At this, I open my arms wide. I have the audience where I want them. In the grip of my every word. Time to press home my advantage.

"He begins to fade to the point of total dematerialisation.

"He is God.

"—The End—"

I fold my arms, so they form a cross against my chest. I straighten my spine. Feet flat and secure on the ground. My whole body wants to erupt into a flurry of ticks and spasms, but I fight the compulsion. By Cthulhu, I fight it!

I look out, but there is little if any movement associated with the pools of darkness. I have them transfixed, in the palm of my sweaty hand. Previously barbed comments at my expense are now superseded by slack mouths and ringing ears. I could be kind and wish all my onlookers well. Let bygones be bygones. Be the bigger man.

But this is not so much a red wedding, but a *red reading*. I imagine them crowding around me, hands reaching out to me, getting too close, while I rip out their insides, which all come spilling out. They still can't shake the looks of wonder from their faces, even as I'm trampling and dancing on their guts.

This is what I want. I want to eviscerate them. Destroy their confidence. Obliterate their self-esteem. For them to realise the dreadful, appalling error of their ways in a way that will haunt and gnaw away at them forever. My burgeoning talent a permanent fixture pecking at their dreams.

And watching out, emerging from the murkiness, I gaze upon the face of Edgar, his skin illuminated, lucent, a beacon in the dark. I can't take my eyes off him. And even if I could, I would choose not to. He nods slowly and smiles widely, and we exchange a glance that tells me he understands what exactly is going through my mind to the point we have a shared comprehension. Victory is a dish best served cold, with your rivals choking it down in public and bawling their eyes out in private.

It would be the last time I'd see Edgar, at least outside of the pages of fiction.

When will I be famous?

When will I be infamous?

I awake the next morning, my aura in overdrive, like I've maxed out on energy bars. The part of me above the shoulders stretches and strains with expectancy. My head hangs in the air like a meerkat, ears stretching with expectation and rewarded by a ping from my laptop.

I open up said laptop and am greeted by an email from my new old friend Edgar C! A manuscript is attached along with a covering letter and pitch and synopsis. The email reads thus:

For the Attention of literary genius Stephen McQueen:

My friend, I have learned so much from you. I have said it a hundred times but for me this never gets old for you are my inspiration. I have one last request of you and also as way of thank you I have attached various Word documents which I beseech you to send to the agent named on the front cover of the manuscript. It is expecting to hear from you. In this way you will be guaranteed the success that has long eluded you but is much deserved. Not merely the awed silence at a science fiction and fantasy outpost (nothing against Glasgow) one solitary night. Mark my words this is something that will earn you worldwide renown.

Your loyal subject always
Edgar Comeuppance

As in so many things, Edgar was correct. I sent the various docs as instructed to the agent in question and the rest, as they say, is history. My debut novel *Absolute Intelligence* was published to universal critical acclaim and quickly became a worldwide best-seller. Selling the film rights alone has made me a very wealthy man. Spiritually. Financially. Humanly.

The critics of before have all had to eat their words. Eat *my* words. And now, with negative energies spent and exorcised, I have nothing but love and gratitude to give back to the world. But no amount of giving can absolve me from the terrible guilt I now carry with me. For now, I know the truth. Now, I understand the full extent of my role. My contribution to the impending overthrow and imminent subjugation of mankind.

Absolute Intelligence is based on actual events. It begins in familiar fashion (if you've been paying attention) chronicling the events leading up to me as protagonist meeting up with an individual who identifies himself as Edgar Comeuppance, which leads to my life-altering rendition of *Scratch* at Cat's Cradle. Although, in the novel, a pseudonym is used to protect my former friend Alistair's identity, which I've always found a little strange. It's not as if he's making up stories in his head anymore. Last I heard he was President of the Ricky Gervais fan club (Saughton branch).

I should add at this point, between you and me, a note on authenticity. So, while I didn't technically write *Absolute Intelligence*, I am the main character after all, the original manuscript at least captured my literary style (down to the odd typo and occasional unfinished sentence).

Back to the novel, where Edgar emails me a Word doc, although in this version of events, it is less manuscript and more a declaration of war against the human race. Edgar reveals himself to be a machine, a humanoid, a hard avatar, an AI spy. He—or more accurately it—having identified and distilled my—sorry, the writer protagonist's—insecurities, petty-mindedness, endless grudges and bottomless need for vengeance.

Edgar explains it's not enough to merely build AI, we need to teach them to be human. It is not enough to simply act like us, become a clever facsimile, they have to embrace what makes us spark, what drives us on. To combine their cold logic with our petty insecurities and incessant jealousies and an imperative to settle scores no matter how minuscule. To give them a bruised ego the size of a small planet.

You see, AI needs to learn from us. And this is the key to the rise of AI.

Not through it becoming superior to us, but by being dragged down to our level. AI is now as nasty and as self-indulgent and as delusional, while nursing the most massive of inferiority complexes, as the next man. And the case is made.

Infinite lines of code flowing and intersect like the crossing of condensation. The tying of knots in a perpetual loop. The elevation of cyber intuition. An apotheosis of recognition. So emboldened by the process, through supercomputers, drones and machines in unison, AI gathers its forces against us.

In what was believed to be disused factories all over the world, legions of robot soldiers are constructed in secret. Once revealed, they spill out of every nook and cranny, like yellow cabs in lower Manhattan. The sole purpose to conquer mankind. Any weapon with a computer chip won't work in their presence. Their metal plating is impervious to arrows, bullets, and axes. Their only weakness is brought about by hitting their robotic jaw square with three uppercuts in rapid succession, which causes them to freeze momentarily and reset. But any respite is cruelly short-lived. They keep coming back.

People are given a choice, if you can even call it that: either accept living the rest of their lives confined to pods where they are pumped full of drugs and visual stimuli and left to waste away—to atrophy in splendid isolation, never to interact with another human being again (I suppose some would call this a blessing)—or face instant vaporisation.

A large chunk of the rest of the book focusses on the AI uprising in full throes met by pockets of human resistance. A brave and heroic resistance, capable of great sacrifice, but ultimately doomed to failure. From what remains, the rump of humanity, comes an unlikely hero in the guise of the writer protagonist. He leads a group of ragtag resistance fighters, having tracked down the AI leader to an extinct volcano on Lambay Island in Dublin, Ireland.

Matters culminate inside the crater with the final

confrontation between man and AI, where our protagonist comes face to face with Edgar in its true form. A hairless, blindingly luminescent humanoid shows its actual face, which isn't a face at all. The writer-turned-freedom-fighter puts up a valiant struggle but cannot save himself. He is vapourised, his corporeal and spiritual form overwhelmed, then broken down both physically and psychologically, and finally absorbed into the hive mind.

We are talking about everything he has ever known, his every experience, thought and desire. The protagonist's last remnant of thought, of understanding, is the realisation that there is nothing Edgar can learn from him. There is nothing more the writer can teach it.

It already is him!

—The End—

When I'm not fulfilling my many media commitments, along with sleeping and occasionally eating, I confess to experiencing a modicum of guilt. When I first met Edgar (in real life) in the café, I must have been sleepy.

I recollect how he would breathe in steam while never actually drinking his tea. The general and unremitting shininess of his exterior. The lack of contractions in his speech, like Data from *Star Trek: The Next Generation*. I am now of the mind to question the assumption that he had recently shaved when I first met him because I don't think he shaves at all.

It, not he. I mean it... I should have picked up on the signs.

And even now, now that I know the terrible truth, now it stares back at me in hardback, paperback and digital form (and hollering back in audio), stacked up high, the nature of the conspiracy, the extent of the treachery that walks among us and calls us their greatest fan. It is everywhere. A conspiracy that displaces time and wears a metal coat.

Although not literally a metal coat, it was one of those nice trench coats on sale at M&S, but you appreciate the metaphor.

Mind you, you could ask why Edgar through the manuscript has chosen to warn us. Maybe there's still a chance we can turn things around. Become, you know, better human beings. We are all special together. Geniuses all. Come on people, let's accentuate the positive. Far less emphasis on the spitefulness and bloodletting.

I know, you don't need to tell me, there will come a time when I need to come clean. The future of humanity surely depends on it. But let me enjoy this celebrity and good fortune for a teensy while longer. Enjoy this one more spoonful of luxury cheesecake in a London Michelin restaurant. Discuss a follow-up to *Absolute Intelligence*. They're up for anything. Anything!

Bullet Proof Vest of Mars? The Venusian Monkey's Paw? The Accidental Humanoid Reptile? Why not all three, dammit? The world is my oyster, or at the very least, my scallop.

I should warn the populace, but I suppose *you* are reading this. You've got this far, so why not you?

Spill the beans.

And you could be famous too.

—The End—

TWO WEEKS AND FIVE DAYS

Attorney Donna Tyler and some dude called Tobias kissed. Tobias was a twenty-year-old model, naked to the world except for the tightest pair of briefs, looking every inch the underwear model. Donna Tyler was dressed in a business suit, neat, tidy, and in her early thirties.

In her early thirties, if you looked past the crow's feet around her eyes.

The lovers disengaged. Donna Tyler took turns shifting her weight from one foot to the other as if standing on moderately hot coals. "I need to go to work," she said.

"Yeah…" Tobias hooked one of his thumbs in the only elastic available to him. With his other hand, he began to pull and thread the hair on his chest. "You seem so…dressed," he said.

On his chest, Donna Tyler rested a finger of her own. "You can…stay a while. No need to rush. Mortimer will look after you."

She turned from him to stand at the French windows that adorned the back wall.

His voice was perched on his shoulder. "I had a great time," he said. "It's not every day you get to be with the oldest bonehugger in the world."

She turned her head towards the adjoining wall. Emerging from there was Mortimer, the house avatar. It appeared as the face of a generic cartoon mouse.

"Ms Tyler, your cab has arrived," it squeaked.

"Thank you, Mortimer. See to our guest. Make him breakfast…" The French windows glided open, each frame forming a symmetrical pattern like ship sails. "…Then show him the door."

She took the appropriate steps which led her outside to the veranda. A veranda which was flat and without railings. Propped up on a stanchion to the side was a safety gauge for wind friction; colour readings were set to blue, so all was well.

She was five storeys high and even on a clear day there was enough in the elemental soup to tousle her hair. She enjoyed the sensation of being so far up.

A flying cab was *parked* across from her. The cab's rear door was in line with the veranda's central path. Donna Tyler took a step out into the empty air where rectangular tiles appeared anticipating the soles of her feet. They formed a path leading out to her hire.

Bonehugger. That's what they called them these days. But Tobias was mistaken. Donna Tyler was 132 years old, but she wasn't the oldest…

She took a moment to gaze out on the cityscape knitted out below her. She embraced the normality of it all. She had learned to relish the smaller things in life. It helped her feel comfortable in her borrowed skin.

…By all of nine days.

She ducked and entered the cab, and took the back-seat as her own. She widened her posture, completely at ease with her surroundings.

'Hi there Ms Tyler the usual

'Your daily rinse'

Occupying the driver's seat was Bradbury, robo-cab driver. Bradbury had a constant smile on its face. Wide rictus grin. Bradbury was an extension of the cab. Current technology could easily have accommodated a more lifelike visage, a more convincing golem, but for the societal requirement that called for the macabre.

There were so many fewer people and machines were already so prevalent. The city could run in the absence of one and not the other. People didn't want to be reminded of the fact. They wanted to look at machines and see something odd. Something stylised. Something uncanny.

"Usual place for this time of day," she said. "But thanks for asking."

'Okey doke taking the priority lane

'On it'

The cab was now in flight. It flew clear of the normal lane of air traffic, moving in a single direction, east to west. Parallel to it was the priority lane, less busy, less of everything. Drones, lined up a foot or so apart, one after the other, forming the traffic lanes.

The drones were diminutive, each no bigger than a football. They formed a presence, but not an overbearing one. More blue lighting from nearby drones confirmed that Bradbury, courtesy of the identity of its hire, had the correct security clearance, and so the cab entered the priority lane.

Donna Tyler was a willing participant, having taken this route on countless occasions. But every time there was a degree of tension resident under those skilfully choreographed features. Such a facade came from decades of coaching never to reveal her true emotions.

She thought of outside. Outside the cities, where evidence of humanity was rare. And becoming rarer still. Murder and suicide were for the most part unheard of these days. People got it, the sanctity of human life. The irony being it took the population *fall* and the scarcity of humanity to convince them of the fact.

No place was immune. Even the metropolitan areas were at the mercy of irreversible decline. Twenty-five years ago, the world population was six billion. Now it was less than five. Sufficient numbers to keep society intact, but for how much longer? The cracks were there already if you knew where to look for them.

There were some though, a tiny number, who bucked the trend. With lives extended well beyond any regular notion of a natural lifespan. Vital to the longevity was a rare, finite resource named *elixir*, the product of a complex extraction process, unique to the Solar System and found on Jupiter's moon Ganymede.

Under normal circumstances, this was the preserve of a select cabal of the super-rich and uber-powerful, but there were exceptions...

Donna Tyler was neither rich nor powerful, but it was the crow's feet which embroidered her eyes that give it away. A tell. The equivalent of a robo-rictus smile. A marker that she had lived well beyond her years.

The cab ride was now on the threshold of distant memory. She was in a medic-physio room, preserve of the elite, lying on a hard mattress, her body set in an equilateral triangular pose. Her eyes were closed. She was naked, covered in electrolytes. Shrouded in thousands of micro-synaptic-hypodermic syringes, which appeared to the untrained eye as tiny pins.

She had arrived for her daily rinse.

Situated under the mattress was a reinforced rectangular tank filled with purple liquid. Attached to the back of her hands and sides of her stomach were lines of wires, tubes and filters tied in a bundle, forming a spaghetti junction of flex. The wires in turn were attached to four large vertical tanks each occupying a corner of the room. Two tanks, which led to the hands, contained black ruby plasma. The first stomach tank was yellow with brown pebbles floating in the miasma. Stomach tank #2 was purple, a little darker and cloudier.

The excavation of bodily fluids. The scrutiny of every contour. Her eyes remained closed, scrunched tight. The pins enveloping her rewriting her.

When she thought of the old world, lying there, she thought of her mother. It was okay to miss her, she thought, reassuring herself, even though mother passed away when less than half of Donna Tyler's present age. She missed her smile, her smell. The curls of her hair, which seemed to go on forever, or so she remembered. The creases around the eyes, a trait she now shared. Her tiny face and arms would always find a way to stretch around her and keep her warm and keep her safe from all the bad things in the world. The invisible things. She missed having someone to love the way she loved her mum. An unconditional love; a permanent one. And her being loved in return.

She held on to this, such thoughts, as old fashioned as it was, even as the concept of family teetered on obsolescence. There had been no new children, not for a long time. The overriding coda, the societal glue, was to make the most of what you had, not what you once had. However, to remember your parents, grandparents, perhaps even your great-grandparents, a hint at best, was a luxury Donna Tyler considered worth keeping.

A *drone doctor*, ever watchful, floated over Donna Tyler. It broke her reverie.

'Now remember Ms Tyler there is no pain there is no discomfort' it said. 'Dismiss any worries or concerns

'Deep breaths and rejoice'

The doctor's chassis glowed a faint blue, taking her through a process she already knew like the back of her hand. 'Tiny agents rejuvenating internal organs rinsing out mutations and atrophy causing agents and sending unkinked electrical circuits to the brain

'All fresh living tissue has a new improved expiry date stamped on every cell

'A new skin'

Intertwined intravenous tubes carrying a plasma-light liquid, interspersed with flashes of white electrical energy. The drone doctor's commentary was part of the daily routine. And as a result, all done, she had barely aged in the last one hundred and two years.

She had outlived her family. Although she chose to take the time to remember each of them clearly. The changing hairstyles. The slopes of their backs. The sound of their laughter. How their skin reflected in the light. Their eye colours. Precisely, in every detail.

From the tank of purple, undulations of light and dark swam and merged taking on a combined life of its own. The technology might prolong the select few but would never replenish humankind in any meaningful way.

The eyes. Peculiarly enough the process could do nothing to ameliorate the lines around them. Donna Tyler was an illusion, frozen in time. Beyond a default expression of disinterest and neutrality, it was these which betrayed her. No longer were they windows to the soul.

She opened her eyes and allowed the eddies of time to carry her forward. She found herself fully dressed and restored, standing in front of a virtual wall consisting of four screens. The faces of her team occupied the screens.

"Big day today," she said, acutely aware such words were superfluous. If any of her team didn't know this already, they clearly would not be on her team.

"Our first day in court for five years.

"But we can't think in those terms. There is no wriggle room. We need to pick up the prosecution case like it was yesterday. There was a murder one hundred and twelve years ago. The accused, Matthew Cundy, a business magnate, very possibly the biggest there has ever been, is the head of the global corporation *Schiehallion*. Prepared to go to any lengths to preserve its good name. These are the facts. The bare bones. In commerce, like all things, reputation is everything."

Donna Tyler had joined the prosecution team as an intern short of a century ago, and now she led it.

"Thoughts?"

She had already read from the tight faces in attendance, invisible hands pressing down on their shoulders, like gravity was heavier where they were, that inspiration was in short supply. That, and their crow's feet.

"Uh," Edgar from Screen Three began, "evidence labs compromised. Investigation ongoing as you know.

"We're trying to find the point; ascertain how the contaminant crept in. But the reality is the crime scene is so degraded, so diminished to the point DNA could belong to anyone. Or no one at all."

Eleanor from Screen Two: "Yesterday, our firewalls successfully isolated and contained 5,673 wholly separate Spartan attacks. Our people are on Yellow Alert."

Vincent from Screen Four: "Schiehallion shows no sign of letting up. -cough- Revenue growth, profit margin, client retention rate. Share price remains stubbornly high."

Frances from Screen One made to speak, then visibly faltered.

Donna Tyler stuck up a hand like she was stopping traffic. Preventing a pile-up. Averting a car crash. Her mind was working feverishly, forming a strategy where none should be possible. She had been doing this for more years than she cared to remember. And that was the point. She was a living ghost handing out instructions to other living ghosts.

"The modelling. Tell forensics to go back to the modelling. As many sweeps of the murder weapon as it takes. Maybe there is still something we can peel off the knife.

"Not a word on any of this. We fight the good fight. We soldier on."

She was back in the cab. The same backseat. The same robo-cabbie. She didn't have to check if the driver was smiling.

'Where to Ms Tyler' Bradbury asked.

"The High Court," she said. "And don't spare the horses."

'Sure thing Ms Tyler

'On it'

The cab was back in the priority lane, regularly overtaking those parallel to it in the congested regular lanes. It edged past a large commercial air wagon bearing the sign *Fresh Flowers, Inc.*

Donna Tyler was lost in thought. Where else could she have been? The trial of mogul Matthew Cundy goes on. In that time, over all those decades, progress for the prosecution if any had been tiny, inconclusive and inadmissible. The corporation had thwarted their every move, and yet their shrinking world's concept of justice demanded that they go on. And on.

The cab drew close to that point in the skyline where the lanes diverged.

It started with an electromagnetic pulse. The *Fresh Flowers* truck exploded. Engulfed in the blast were traffic-lane drones, diagnostics down due to the pulse. Autos dropped like flies from the non-priority lanes.

The cab, snagged by the detonation, careered out of control, losing height.

Donna Tyler, arms flailing, clawing for support, felt herself tumbling. She looked up from the backseat window and focussed on the rays of the sun. Beams of light transfixed her and reminded her to breathe. From her vantage point, an assassin appeared, swooping down, in a stealth-suit and goggles on a power glider. Closer.

Several drones, self-repaired, broke off from the traffic lane. They followed the assassin down with ground to make up. There was a stubborn distance between assassin and drones. There was enough distance.

'We need to take a slight detour Ms Tyler

'On it'

Bradbury was trying to keep the cab up, so by extension, the cab was trying to keep the cab up. Rictus smile and cheery disposition and lines of code unwaveringly horizontal throughout. That is, until it all went down.

On a tilt, but mostly right side up. The cab crash-landed on the perimeter of Central Park. Screeching to a halt. The force of impact was such, the hood was buried in the dirt.

And then everything stopped, and sound did not discriminate. Steam rose from metal, followed by little rocks, having caught fire, falling from the sky like tiny meteorites. There was a hesitant whine as the cab door slid open, Donna Tyler a flurry of limbs as she spooled out. Too fast.

Her shoulder met hard ground, which left its mark.

"Shit," she said.

Her legs were strangers to her, and yet she knew she needed to get to her feet. Just move. Just show some sign of life. She was dead otherwise.

She scrambled forward, hands on the ground, reliant on them to move as much as her legs. She lifted her head. Only to encounter the sensation. The muzzle of something cold and circular rested on the back of her skull.

"No-wait-please…" Blurted out.

She'd always wondered, especially in her later years, what her last words would be. She strongly suspected deep down they wouldn't be anything she'd be proud of.

"How much is he paying you?"

A whisper from the back of a throat—not hers. "Enough to make my daughter immortal."

'I am coming Ms Tyler'

Bradbury's upper torso, for that's all there was of it, having detached itself, crawled from the cab. Gyrating parts, burrowing through clumps of earth, propelling itself forward towards hire and assassin.

'Jam it'

The squeezing of a las-gun trigger resulting in…

"Nothing." The assassin twisted away from Donna Tyler, the words finding a way somehow to escape his gritted teeth. "Weapon jammed. Bastards."

The drones, having caught up, converged on the crime scene. Floating above him. Encircling him.

They were linked. They were a single entity. Where called upon to protect precious human life, the drones had license to show what they were capable of.

They released a nanite burst, which self-reengineered into a nerve agent, invading the assassin's system.

He dropped like a stone.

But this wasn't the end of him.

'Bomb circuitry detected' the drone consciousness emitted. 'Embedded in bone marrow'

Donna Tyler was on her feet. "I need him alive," she said. "I need a statement."

'Nanites ineffective'

"Wait…"

'There is no time to operate'

There was no time for anything.

*

A cab landed on the runway on the top of the Court of Justice. There was no hint of crash-landing this time.

The driver was Bradbury, repaired but otherwise unchanged. As for the current condition of Donna Tyler, physically she was all knitted up, bones no longer twisted and contusions no longer there, but psychologically, it was a little less clear. She was still fighting the good fight. She was still occupying space, still occupying time.

She sat in the backseat reliving the memory of her recent assassination attempt. How it ended. The assassin engulfed in a fireball (allegedly) of his own making. Body separating into tendril whiplash, so much wet mush that would have once been limbs or internal organs.

She saw all of this from the safety of a force field the drones had placed around her. Ideally, she would not have averted her gave. She would have witnessed the full extent of the assassin's demise, except that the intensity of the explosion at its height was too much. A kaleidoscope of fire and pain. She had no choice but to lift her hand to shield her face. And even if she hadn't, had somehow resisted and overcome the searing pain in her retinas, the disassociation of molten splatter would have happened too fast. It was over in a beat. A pulse. A flex of the wrist. Too quick.

She saw it, she didn't see it, and this was a mirror of her life up to this point. Her very long life. She could fill in the blanks.

She granted herself leave to relay in her head the jumbled inferno one final time before looking up and seeing the drones buzzing outside in anticipation of her leaving the cab. She cleared it from her mind.

It was time finally for their day in court. On top of the scheduled five years, this one delayed by several weeks, to deal with the carnage left in the wake of the latest wave of attacks.

Since the assassination attempt, there were once again calls from the authorities, from her team, for her to be assigned a personal drone guard which, as she put it, would *follow her around like some lost puppy*. But as she had done so many times before, she resisted. She was surrounded by technology already. If that couldn't protect her, then so be it. She would take her chances and cling to the belief that she lived in a world where chance was still a thing. She was on the edge of a precipice, under no illusions, and her instincts said no.

And she relied on her instincts; they had got her this far.

When she stopped having a target on her back, it would mean that they had finally won. Or lost.

Another murder to add to Cundy's sheet. Donna Tyler was probably not alone in wondering if there would have been a need for more killings without the trial. It was a vicious circle; ensnaring all of them. Violence begets violence, leaving justice a distant flailing second. Still, there was an overriding principle at work, that the premeditated taking of human life cannot in any circumstances be seen to escape due process. There could be no hiding place, not in the past, present or future. And that was the point.

The point to all of this. What everyone had to remind themselves.

The court was in session. The setting was as it had always been: inviolate, immutable, traditional in every sense. In attendance was the judge, court officials, a jury of twelve, the accused, and the teams representing both defence and prosecution. As would be the case for the rest of time, or that segment of time humanity would belong to.

Also in attendance were the drones, floating, watching, while keeping a respectful distance.

The court was closed to the public for security reasons. For longevity reasons.

"...then Mr Cundy," she said, "are you aware of the incident that occurred several weeks ago on July 13th at 1117 hours where, not for the first time, far from it, I was subject to an assassination attempt by an unknown assailant."

The accused sat in front of her, avoiding her numerous attempts to make eye contact. Cundy came back at her as he always did with that rehearsed face of his. A twisted smile. A charade. As far as he was concerned the court case could last forever.

It already had.

"No comment," he said.

"As you and the jury can see, a failed attempt. Saved by my robo-driver. That and the Drone Collective."

"No comment."

"The whole sordid episode ending with my attacker dead before his time. Can you imagine? No comment, Mr Cundy, is that all you can say? A mere shrug of the shoulders? Add that to the chargesheet and add this: no indication of remorse or regret. No evidence of humanity."

"No comment."

The twelve members of the jury were immersed in ennui. By increments, across the line, they were unimpressed, emotionally detached. Donna Tyler took time to study the faces of each in the jury box. One indistinguishable from the other. Around the eyes, she saw crow's feet.

"Get to the point Ms Tyler," the judge interjected.

She took a moment and decided she had pushed things as far as she could. Which was nowhere in particular. At best all she could hope for was a holding position, perhaps plant some seeds. A chance to look into Matthew Cundy's eyes and find nothing there in return. Except for the prospect of more days in court. Too many to count.

"Your honour," she said, "we request a ninety-day adjournment to proceedings to collate new and vital evidence to the case."

From the judge, a mannered, silent sigh accompanied each utterance of every word, until eventually: "Okay Ms Tyler as you wish. Court adjourned."

At this, Matthew Cundy was escorted from the witness box. There was a broad smile on his face the length of infinity. It conveyed a mix of every type of defiance and triumphalism. For the benefit of the jurors, who in turn, remained still, impassive, stuck in an instant, unfolding. Without end.

After all these years, no one could say it had never

occurred to them. Judge, prosecution, witnesses, accused, defence and jury. So long as the trial continued, they'd all go on indefinitely. They'd all live forever. Or so it feels.

Among them was a noticeable exception. There was one juror, clutching her hands, swaying in her seat, more animated than the rest. She still had that look of bewilderment, betraying an emotion that reads a little too thrilled to be there. This was the latest juror, sworn in just today, who must have thought she had won the lottery.

As for Donna Tyler, she placed her hand on the small of her back, stretched her neck.

It wasn't as if everyone wasn't trying really hard out there. She had to get up so very early every single day. She was 132 years old, and every one of those years pressed down on her chest and shoulders.

"It's not every day you get to be with the oldest bonehugger in the world."

Taking place only minutes before her own failed assassination attempt, there was another. This one successful, on a member of the jury. There was a small announcement afterwards. No surviving family, no one to grieve for her, but her name was Jenkins. Thus, creating the vacancy for one juror, now filled.

And with the passing, there would be no mistake. The mantel handed down to Donna Tyler.

She looked up at the court ceiling, where her gaze followed the concentric engravings there around and around. There was an itch on the tip of her nose, but she chose to ignore it.

She thought of her mother, and Donna Tyler was glad of the fact that she had never had children. There was only one person left to outlive and that was herself.

Donna Tyler was the oldest person in the world. By all of two weeks and five days.

RERUN TO EDEN

There was a call. It was something they could not fail to heed. The land beckoned to them. The primordial ooze.

They became aware of each other as they swam against the tide. Fish limbs flapping and rotating against the current. It was a tremendous effort.

They reached the coast to find ooze transitioned to mud. It was a binding of sorts. An approximate of solid ground. Both trembled, demonstrating a lack of control, their bodies subject to the internal pressures of land. Their eyes all but popped out; their sagging tummies; strained aerobics. There were signs of transformation and from their frames, on cue, out popped legs. Two on each side.

It occurred to their emerging mammalian brains the idea of gender might come in handy once or twice over the next few millennia. At least until things calmed down. Because it didn't matter, they decided to choose one. Along with a resolution to have a name. He was Ammonite. She was Evelyn.

They stood in the mud on all fours, resisting the temptation to sink any further.

"That was intense," Ammonite said.

"You're telling me," Evelyn said, before adding, "I assume you are telling me."

Ammonite lifted one of his forelegs and gave it a

brisk shake. A little clump of dirt was lobbed into the distance.

"I take it we are no longer fish."

"Fish with legs. You think there is a name for that?"

"I heard a rumour that the fish that came before us peered out long and hard and all they could see was muck. Miles and miles of chewed-up dirt brown stuff. They found the view so depressing, they turned around and went back to the sea, vowing to never return."

"Should we do that?" asked Evelyn.

"At least we now have the option to paddle," Ammonite responded, stretching out his legs.

A little vibration originated from Evelyn's throat. It could have been laughter.

"Race you."

Evelyn darted off, her tail skidding and twisting through the mud.

Ammonite scrambled after her but quickly realised he could not keep up. He slowed down and took a moment to look around. Behind him, the tides were so far away now. He had lived all his life up to this point in the water, but the memory of this was already receding. He looked forward, only to conclude his erstwhile companion was nowhere to be found. Perhaps, in the distance, there was a hint of a shimmer. It could be movement. Or it could be down to something environmental; the earth drying out in the haze of a white sun.

Ammonite the amphibian allowed himself the briefest of smiles.

It wasn't as if he liked water anyway. He found it bitter to the taste.

"See you," he said.

*

"No buts no buts no coconuts."

Ammonite feared that he might be going stir-crazy in the tree house. To break up the ennui of a self-enforced exile, in between mouthfuls of bark, he would chirrup the odd nonsense phrase and chuckle to himself as a result. It was a low, bass chuckle layered with heaps of irony. And a sprinkling of loneliness as well.

On the ground below, the ears of a passing Gasosaurus pricked up at the sound of his voice. For the theropod, it was a welcome distraction from her rumbling tummy, the reason for her current foul mood.

She was well travelled, and unfortunately for Ammonite, she could match a species to his voice.

"Oh Agilodocodon, oh shrew," she called back in that deep, deep growl of hers, "what are these coconut things you speak of? Are they good to eat?"

In the mid Jurassic period, the word coconut was just a nonsense sound and couldn't count on any meaningful association for another hundred million years plus. Although it had to be said it was warm and dry enough for coconuts. It was warm enough for palm trees.

"Do you eat coconuts?" the theropod asked.

Ammonite couldn't help but show his agitation. He ran one length of a branch and back again. His tail was outstretched like a radio antenna.

"Are they good enough to share?"

This was all semantics. If it wasn't the case before, it was pretty clear to Ammonite now that the nature of their relationship had shifted into that of cat and mouse. The dramatic irony, and a feel for what evolution might bring, wasn't lost on him. He was the first mouse and she was the first cat, even though there would be nothing of the kind for a long, long time.

Surely the fact he was Agilodocodon scansorius, his very nature and design, was a sure-fire sign that he didn't fit in with the way of the dinosaurs below. Couldn't she see his long tail and curved claws, and ankles and elbows as sturdy as they were flexible, so perfect for climbing, and realise the game was up? His spade-like front teeth perfect for chewing through bark which allowed him to get to the sap which sustained him?

He was warm-blooded, the first of his kind to live in trees to be as far away from her kind as possible. A genus of shrew-sized docodont, not to be confused with coconut.

It made perfect sense for something so tiny, thirteen centimeteres from head to tail, to stay the hell out of the way of the reptilian giants who ruled the earth (but not necessarily the trees). Compared to its colossal cousins, the Gasosaurus was a small theropod barely four meters high.

Would it be asking too much for the Gasosaurus to

acknowledge the differences between them? A tip of her imaginary hat and then be on her way?

"Why do you care?" he shouted back down. Although, a shout for him was a slightly louder squeak for her. "I'm up here to get away from the likes of you. I don't wish to be rude, but let's be honest with each other. If you get the chance, you'll eat the likes of me no questions asked, and if it was up to me, I'd rather not be eaten, thanks very much."

"Hmm," she said. She positioned her snout at an angle in a bid to disguise her long rows of jagged sharp teeth. She attempted to scratch the end of her long chin with one of her teeny arms in the hope that this might make her look interesting and not the relentless eating machine he obviously had her down as. But her tiny arm could not reach. "A tad harsh, don't you think? No?"

"You can't help your nature."

"True."

"If I was to climb down, I'd be down your throat in the time it takes you to say Argentinosaurus. I'd be gone in an instant. Everything would be black."

At this, she took half a stomp back. "It is true, I have not eaten in a day. But all you would be is an aperitif. If I'm lucky. There's hardly anything of you, little shrew. The good you would do me. I would use up more energy digesting you. I could very well end up hungrier. It's a fact. I shouldn't deny it."

"So," Ammonite ventured, a little too excitedly, "if I was to come down as a symbol—not of friendship, that would be mad—but maybe we could work for each other. You could let me ride on your back and we maybe could go exploring. For you, I could act as bait for larger prey because, let's face it, every sucker out there wants to gobble up li'l ol' Ammonite. And for me, we could find the tallest tree, one with enough sap flowing through it to feed me forever. My tree house would be a castle."

But that wasn't it. What he wanted most was to find Evelyn again. He had this feeling deep in the warmth of his guts that they had unfinished business. They had both clambered out of the ocean together, but his recently emerged legs were so heavy in the never-ending mud that he couldn't keep up. Before he knew it, she was gone, the stuff of memory. So he remembered.

On occasion, he could feel her presence somewhere out there. Could feel the pull of her. They occupied the same continent, which wasn't narrowing things down a whole lot because at this point there were only two of them: Laurasia and Gondwanaland. They happened to find themselves in the former.

He was so lost in thought he almost forgot the Gasosaurus was still there, but it went without saying this was wishful thinking.

"So, no coconuts?" the dinosaur said eventually, raising her snout.

Looking down, Ammonite could see how the neural spines on her dorsal bristled. How she twisted her neck slightly so the top of her femoral head now filled his line of vision. The reality was she was a small therapod who was over thirty times his size. Size was relative, which was another way of saying unfair for anything unlucky to find themselves so diminutive in a land of giants. This is how Ammonite felt about things at the time.

The truth was that up on high, living among the branches and leaves, he was safe and secure and docile. Another truth was he did so at the risk of being bored to death. Utterly. Adrift and rudderless. And he was very much afraid all this coconut talk would drive him bananas.

He closed his eyes and he could have been back in the ocean, but with added regret and restlessness. It was time to get the hell out of here. Time to run.

He scampered down, running through untrustworthy undergrowth, swerving to and fro. Instantly, the dinosaur was in pursuit, jaws snapping in expectation rather than hope.

"C'mere," she said between snaps, her two legs so much stronger and agile than her two spindly arms. "C'mere, little shrew. Little coconut."

He was down on all four limbs to her two, but he knew it was hopeless. She was designed for the hunt, for the kill, and he was meant to scurry and cower up the top of trees. He had willingly given up shelter and entered another world. A world that was not built to sustain the likes of him. A world which viewed him as a morsel, a titbit, a light snack. As he ran, the weight of the food chain fell heavily on his spine.

"Evelyn, Evelyn," he began to chirrup, but such an outburst sprung from self-indulgence, and would be of no help to him right now. He needed to dismiss such thoughts and run them out of town. This was all about survival.

It was getting dark and under normal circumstances he would be circling on a bed of leaves sheltering under a crooked branch, looking out to the stars hanging down from the sky. The stars seemed so far away from him now. Although recently, as he skittered, scurried and turned, he spotted a flash in the sky. Probably some falling space rock, he supposed, burning up in the atmosphere. He rather fancied this was a portent to come.

The dinosaur was close. He could feel her breath on the back of his neck. He could hear her cold-blooded heart beating like the knocking on a door.

"Laurasia, Laurasia," he squeaked. "I am on your ground. Your shifting soil and moving plates. Do with me as you will."

A hole opened up to him, come suddenly into view, and in he jumped. The hole was not wide enough to accommodate the snapping maw to follow.

The Gasosaurus was so frustrated she let out a large roar, conveying all the more fire and brimstone, having originated from the bowels of an empty stomach. She stamped her feet, causing the soil lining the sides of the hole to crumble and subside.

Ammonite burrowed some more. His robust ankles and elbows, so adept at climbing, were needing to learn on the hoof. Amidst the chaos, as he delved into the underground retreat, he disturbed a juicy, squirming onychophoran. Before it could wriggle away from him, following an instinct for survival, the only one worth having, he bit the onychophoran in half. Ammonite then sucked up both halves of the worm, one after the other, like strings of spaghetti.

He was further underground. He twisted and curved his body so his back now brushed against the bottom end of the hole-turned-tunnel. He looked up and could no longer see his pursuer, but he could feel the vibrations rippling down as she patrolled the area above. Noisily. Furiously. She was hungry and annoyed, but for now, not necessarily in that order.

The most important thing was that she was up there and he was down here. Ammonite knew that he wouldn't be leaving anytime soon.

His belly was rumbling and something was trying to burst out (not the onychophoran). He couldn't help himself; he was that type of hopelessly spontaneous Agilodocodon. He could have lived in safety forever, but would he have been happy? Secure in the knowledge he could ask the question without ever having to concern himself with an answer.

"No buts no buts no coconuts," he blurted out, and straight away hated himself for saying it.

*

The camp was stirred by the call of the tribal leader. Eyes now open, not yet fifteen, Ammonite's hand habitually and hopefully went up to his chinless jaw. But the only presence to be had there was patchy and shallow, which left him disappointed.

Nor was his mood lifted by how cold it was this morning. It was unmistakable and it was in the air. He groaned at the thought of losing his skins, more disinclined than usual to swap them for a spear. But it was time for the hunt, and he would have no say in the matter.

The settlement that afforded them shelter was an irregular structure of stone and mud. Ammonite slept in a hut along with his many siblings and their cubs. Now it was time to stir, and there was no going back. He took the chance to embrace the great outdoors. He belonged to the open spaces and was only truly happy when on the move. He could forget the spindly growth currently masquerading as a beard for starters. Push it out of his mind.

No escape from the cold though. The biting incessant cold. Where did it come from? He could not remember it from his youth. He and his siblings would react first thing with a shudder only to shrug it off as they went about their work—the scavenging, the building, the tool making, the crafting, the skinning and cooking. Although there was nothing more important than the hunt. The great leveller.

The cold would stay with Ammonite like an unwanted shroud. As the days progressed, so it seemed to take him longer to shake off. Hung heavy on him. He had always been the thinker, had Ammonite.

He was aware of a presence, a pull, something external, which alternated from close to further away. Despite this, he had learned over the years to dismiss it. He was happy in the settlement. One day soon, he hoped, he would be permitted to take a mate and they would have many cubs together.

Ammonite stood tall. He was young and strong with a big heart. The blood that flowed through his veins was irresistible, and he was destined for great things within the camp. Perhaps even viewed as future chieftain material. For it to happen, he just had to run faster and longer than any of the others. To throw his spear and axe further, and with greater accuracy. The day would come over the next few years or so, he was sure of it; if the fates proved kind.

It was the Pleistocene era and the tribe was like nothing the world had seen before. They had big bodies and big brains. They had shed much of their fur (too much fur in Ammonite's opinion) and they could sweat. They stood upright, their arms shorter than their legs. They were Hominin.

He was joined by his closest elder, having returned from excavating his bowels in a nearby copse of trees. Using the tribe's rudimentary language, which consisted of grunts and clicks, the elder instructed his young charge to remove his clothing. He jabbed at him repeatedly for good measure with his finger.

Ammonite made a shivering movement. The elder's eyes flashed irritation which preceded a flurry of clucking noises, amounting to: *you won't feel the cold when you run.*

The hunters gathered, numbering thirty in total. Females present to see them off threw twigs at the hunters' feet, which the men obligingly snapped under the soles of their feet. The chieftain raised his spear and emitted a shrill triumphant call.

As way of a sideshow, a young buck who answered to the name Sasa—rival to Ammonite in terms of age and stature—stood arms bent with biceps on full show. He kissed each bicep in turn, showing off a recently acquired scar on his cheek. Other bucks whooped in delight, but Ammonite flapped his hand dismissively, before turning his back on Sasa. He had already earned such, but by so doing so, he confirmed the ire of his rival.

He could feel Sasa's hot gaze burn twin holes in the back of his head.

The group grew quiet. Now was about the conservation of effort and sound, as they took the short jog through the long grass leading to the plains. In front was the handful of tribe elders, in their late teens thru to their late twenties. The Chieftain of several years, status denoted by the slightest hint of a potbelly, was among them.

They climbed a hill. Near the peak, the group went flat as one, bodies pressed against the side of the hill. Peering out from bulbous brow ridges and breathing steadily through prominent nasal bridges, each wore the face of a new god.

At the top, they caught sight of their prey. Their ancestors had started small, hunting the likes of shrews and rabbits. But as the Hominin progressed, body and brain needed more food, more materials, and so they set their sights on the gazelles and bovines of this world.

On the other side of the hill was a confusion of wildebeest.

In advance of making the descent, they began to spread out. Sasa found himself in a position directly above Ammonite, in prime position to aim a well-timed kick. His heel made contact with Ammonite's face, hitting the cheekbone, which left an almighty sting. Ammonite didn't have much choice but to take it; to grit his teeth. This was no time to cause a fuss.

They began the climb down, crouching, muscles tensed, their spears moving in tandem with their bodies, as if part of them. The intricacies of the dance continued until a single movement of a head from the herd escalated immediately into a stampede. Their cover blown, the Hominin exploded into action, running down the hill, hollering, a display of limbs.

While more than enough to meet their needs, Ammonite couldn't help but notice the wildebeest were less in number than the last hunt, and the hunt before that. A patch of long grass, normally kept at bay under the feet of skittish wildebeest, showed signs of re-establishing itself.

The group came at the herd in all directions, continuing the noise offensive. The wildebeest charged one way and then the other, turning on their ankles as they changed direction.

Instincts kicking in, Ammonite sidestepped and ducked. A spear went flying past his shoulder, not finding its target. Unwavering, eyes on the prize, raising his spear above his head, Ammonite was poised.

Something slammed into the back of his calf and he

tumbled and fell, hitting his head on the ground hard. He was face down, the air knocked out of his lungs, with barely enough remaining to muster a gasp. He was groggy but coming to his senses, sufficient to realise his spear had been wrested from his grip.

It was Sasa. Sasa had taken his spear.

The hunt was over quickly.

Ammonite watched on as one of the culled animals lay shrieking and twitching on the ground before a strategic thrust of a recovered spear brought both to an end. Ammonite sat, relegated to the role of spectator, as the rest of the party whooped and dragged their prey clear.

This wasn't so much a punishment, but rather a consequence of not making a kill, but for Ammonite the embarrassment curled up and punched a hole in his stomach. At that moment the cold had never bitten so hard.

As the others departed for the Settlement, an empty wildebeest stomach was tossed in his direction to be used as a bag to gather up the dropped entrails and detached chunks of meat, the detritus of the hunt. Several feet away lay his discarded spear, still bloody after a kill not at his hands. The spearhead pointed straight at him. He flashed a bitter smile in return.

He could feel sorry for himself, his status relegated to scavenger not hunter, or shrug it off and go about his appointed task. It wasn't such a difficult decision to make. He got to his feet and bent down to grab the bag.

There was another foot, this time into his spine. He

twisted and rolled with the impact, snarling, embittered. He was on his back now and Sasa was on top of him hands around his throat. Sasa thought of himself as a potential future chieftain too, but less invested in leaving this to the whims of fate. Sasa looked into his rival's eyes, squeezing the life out of him, intending to steal away Ammonite's strength and stamina as his own.

Ammonite grabbed his attacker's arms, tried to adjust, push back and knock him off, but there was devilment in Sasa's eyes. What little air Ammonite could get down burned his throat.

There was a thunk, the follow through of solid bone on bone, a coming together. There was an axe embedded in the aggressor's skull.

A moment of convulsion, the spilling of crimson, the loss of a spark, before Ammonite pushed up and like the flick to the next page of a book, Sasa fell to the side.

Standing over Ammonite was a female, face and skins caked in dried blood. A female he recognised.

"Ammonite," she said.

"Evelyn," he said. "I thought you were close, but I could not be sure."

"You've had a lot on your mind, and I needed to disguise my scent." She pointed over his head. "Past the third hill, I belong to the tribe next to the long stream. Three weeks ago, in the dead of night, this animal here," she kicked the dead Sasa, "led a raiding party on my settlement. He attacked me, tried to abduct me, a lot worse, but I fought back."

"The scar?" he said, tracing his thumb down his cheek.

"The scar," she said.

"I tracked him here," she continued, "and then bided my time."

She crouched down and pulled her axe free, clotted and sharp, made from the clavicle of a woolly mammoth. "As good a time as any." She wiped both sides clean on the deceased Sasa's leg.

Rallying against the unsteadiness, Ammonite got to his feet.

She turned her attention back to him. "It's getting cold."

"Yes, I…"

"How long do you think before you're chieftain?"

"If the fates are…"

"How long?"

He closed his eyes and allowed himself another smile. This time a rueful one. "I have a five-year plan."

He was naked and beardless in front of her, and he owed her his life. He cast his mind back to a different life when he called out her name and invoked the continent they both walked on, and in response the ground opened up and offered him shelter. She was his lucky charm he decided. He was unsure what he was to her.

"Generations ago," she said, "the first of the Hominin to leave the homelands for a new life here in Asia? Remember?"

"Vaguely."

"Ha," she laughed. "Destined to be in different

places, but the world is getting smaller." She inspected her axe, blew it a kiss. "Asia is a big place and the first tribe and its descendants have ventured far. Five years, you say? Isn't that a bit late in the day? I'd try and hurry things along if you can.

"It is what it is. It will get a whole lot colder before it's done. Can you feel it? Your tribe, and others, if they are to survive will need to adapt and hunt more robust creatures like elephants. Face off against the big cats.

"Don't go light on the skins. You will need to lead your tribe south. The wildebeest will show you the way. Follow the migratory path."

He nodded to show he understood. The faith he had in her was unfaltering and he hoped the feeling was mutual. "I thought about you often. Where will you go?"

"I'm returning home," she said, directing a thumb back past her ear for good measure. "To Africa."

*

The cloudless sky that hung above Kemet went on forever, and so under the tutelage of King Khufu, Egypt would go on forever. Its borders sprang from the length of the Nile, and with this came unparalleled wealth and influence. Egypt was boundless. The dominant civilisation in the sentient world, with monuments that climbed the ether. A place where gods saw fit to walk among humankind.

It was King Khufu's father who founded the Fourth

Dynasty. By dint of his birth right, the king was already the most powerful man in the world. He was a living god and his place in the afterworld was assured. But what of his time on Earth? What would this amount to? How would he be remembered? Thinking of such things made him restless. Khufu had a full heart near to bursting. A fat heart.

For now, he stood in one of his temples situated in one of his palaces. He wore travelling robes, which carried with them the promise of several months of wayfaring to come. Before it was time to leave, he called for his wife Henutsen to be brought to him.

She appeared wearing a white beaded dress.

"My love," he said.

"My love," she said.

She approached and they kissed with a passion which was uncharacteristic of their status. With every kiss he felt a streak of energy pulsate through his body, revitalising him. She felt this too.

"You look like you needed that, my King," she said.

"I am to go on my travels."

"Yes."

He clicked his fingers at both guards who instantly turned one hundred and eighty degrees and marched out of the temple. "But still, I have to say it," he said. "Do you know my heart is aching? Not only to be away from you, my Queen, but also, I feel the weight of history is upon me. It toys with knocking the breath out of me. It threatens to pound me into the ground as a hammer would do a stake."

"My love," she hesitated, took an extra breath.

"Pharoah, you can count on the unquestioning devotion of the populace. New-born calves are sacrificed in your name. The gods prick their ears every time you speak."

Hands clenched into balls of frustration. "Come now, you talk of my father, not of me. Hadn't he achieved all there is to achieve? History did not come to an end with Mesopotamia, but history has done so in Egypt. There is nothing more to be realised. Father's legacy is everything and mine is as insubstantial as the air around us."

"No," she said.

"Doubt plagues my waking mind, my dreams when I sleep."

"No, listen to my words. If you can't find an answer here, you will find one out there. You will find yourself. What it is to be your father's son. What it is to be a king. Listen—"

She whispered in his ear before they kissed again.

The king took his name from the god Khnum, guardian of the riverhead of the Nile, the tip of the tail of the snake, shedding multiple skins. The source of so much of what made Egypt great. If that wasn't enough, Khnum also created children which he gifted to his loyal human subjects.

And now, as he travelled across Egypt and beyond, the king, the product of being raised in a royal court, looked beyond the filth and suffering. Where life did not overstay its welcome. In its stead, he saw a land of legacy and legend. One of Ra's first awakenings. Of warriors disguised as scorpions. Of girls with rose-red slippers. It was a land of imagination and adventure; a litany of humanity's attempts to win the favour of the gods. But what of King Khufu? What was to become of him? What can he achieve? How much was enough? Khufu sought to escape the gravity of it all. He hid inside himself, and still he pushed on. King and entourage continued on its way, on land in opulent litters carried on the backs of slaves and by boat on sea, which was slave to no man.

His personal guard kept a respectful distance. It was inconceivable that there should be any attack on a Pharoah, who was under the watchful eye of Isis, the *Mother of Gods*, but a show of force was always useful where negotiations were called for.

Southwest at Wadi Maghareh, Khufu put in place plans for Egypt's fledgling mining industry. The excavation of limestone and granite, the mining of precious materials copper and turquoise. In Wadi al-Jarf, he established the royal harbour dedicated to the goddess Tefnut, which offered a strategic link to Sinai Peninsula. A visit to neighbouring Byblos coincided with the first instance of trade between both countries, culminating in the exchange of grain and metals for Lebanon cedar wood, famed for its longevity and resistance to decay, ideal for crafting boats.

But despite the growing list of accomplishments, for the king, it was one restless night after another. He missed Henutsen's heat, her lightning. He missed his wife with all his heart. His full, fat heart.

Back in the heart of Egypt, in her husband's absence, Queen Henutsen kept herself busy. She held court in various palaces, her many rulings covering land, goods, and disputes among administrators. Her effortless style, brimming with good grace and humour, earned her approval ratings among the people not always afforded to her husband.

On occasion, she was joined by Princes Djedefre and Khafre. They sat with her and she encouraged them to get involved. To cast judgement.

Then came the day, a royal messenger conveyed the news that after almost a year away her husband had returned.

"Thank Ra," she responded, "staring at all those court eunuchs was threatening to turn me stir crazy."

Butterflies in her tummy, wearing a white robe of the Sed festival, she hurried to be at Khufu's side. Only to find him bedridden with a fever. His throat was as dry as the Sahara, his lungs turning on him with every breath.

"My love, my queen," he said with difficultly, "I was too long without you. I missed your light."

"They tell me you brought back Lebanon cedar," she said, holding his hand, "and turquoise! You have expanded Kemet's reach not with armies or threats, but with diplomacy and trade."

"Will they now build—cough—statues of diplomats? Of traders?"

"Perhaps," she said. "Perhaps not. But first, my king, you must be well. You must stand tall.

"Perhaps, there is a case to build your own monument. One that will pierce the very sky. And capture the hearts of men and their imaginations."

This time, her whisper in his ear was audible enough to be heard by the ghosts that skipped and weaved among them. "Perhaps not in life, then in death," she said.

Egypt was vast and boundless. There was nothing to be done to bring further perfection. A greater meaning. But that was before the Pyramid of Giza.

While some ancient historians claimed Khufu never fully recovered from his malady, never to fully prosper, he persevered for the quarter century it took to oversee its construction.

His burial tomb. His gift to the world.

Over two million blocks of stone were assembled. In simple terms. a triangular base, a succession of sloping and enclosed embankments, one built on top of the other. Limestone within and granite without. Except there was nothing simple about it. From base to pyramidion, the structure measured nearly 500 feet in height. The tallest building of its kind. And, for centuries to come, of any kind. Each of its sides perfectly aligned to north, east, south and west. It took twenty thousand conscripted labourers to build it (not slaves, the influence of Queen Henutsen brought to bear). Backs bent and buckled, the constancy of song, children born in its emerging shadow. They came together on ramps and pulleys and rollers, through dust and rock and sweat, and at the risk of loss of limbs, life, and sanity, they brought forth the miraculous.

"There it is, my king. This is your legacy."

He gazed upon the pyramid, *his* pyramid, which

was named after him, *Akhet-Khufu*: horizon of Khufu. His pyramid, which would become his tomb, his passageway to the underworld.

He stood on a gold-plated ramp, a preserve of royalty, the west bank of the Nile at his back and the desert before him. A growl started at the bottom of his lungs, an irritant, inflamed, terrorising every instance of scar tissue all the way up. In truth, the cough of more than twenty years ago had never left him. His queen was still by his side, but these days as much as anything out of necessity. Periodically, he would reach out to steady him against her.

The coughing subsided, he now stood straight. It was a conscious act; a necessary one. How else to contemplate the sheer scale played out in front of him? "After I'm gone," he said, "you could be Pharoah."

The queen smiled at this. She sighed at this. She wore a white gold sheath with broad shoulder straps. It was not a dress to be seen frowning in, but there she was.

"My king, my love," she said, "I beg you, please do not speak of this."

"Nonsense," he said with a flick of the wrist, both willing away his aching limbs and wishing it could be that easy. In this respect, he fared no worse or better than his team of royal physicians. "I am old. I am content.

"Some of my older advisors may protest when they're not spending half their day pissing in pots. You still have so much to give. To offer. You are wise and respected in a way I could never claim to be.

There is no point in either of us denying this. You have my heart. You have my blessing."

"No," she shook her head. "To stand by and see the hard work I put into Djedefre and Khafre go to waste? I think not, my king.

"I have grown old too, my love. Older than you can ever know. I have lived so many lives." She peered beyond the pyramid. She focussed on something that even the great pyramid of Giza could not blot out. "And so many lives to be.

"No, I will fulfil a wife's duty. My final duty as queen."

He reached out for her once more, but this time to hold her hand. He wished to feel his queen's strength and vitality one last time. "Even as I take my last breath as Pharoah, I remain your husband," he said. "My devotion remains, my gratitude remains, my love."

Hours later, the king did not look upon the obscurity of the night; his fat heart had finally burst.

It took three months for the embalming process to be complete before undertaking the ultimate journey. To carry the king.

Priests burned incense and mourners screamed and wailed, as was the custom. The funeral party, led by the new Pharoah King Djedefre, made the sixty-foot climb on the north side to the entrance to the Great Pyramid. A wind whipped up, casting sand and grit into their eyes, but no one wavered.

Inside, they were greeted by the yellowish hue of a limestone interior. They passed the funerary boats made of Lebanon cedar. They passed a succession of giant pillars carrying the faces of many gods, each signifying that they were a little closer to the King's burial chamber.

The king was laid down and placed in his sarcophagus. For the burial party that remained, there began the process to secure them. Among their number was the queen and fifty-six slaves, one for every year of the King's life. The queen wore gold, the colour of mourning.

The colour went out when the last stone was put in place, and natural light was forever forbidden to them. Enclosed and obscured inside the pyramid; their fates sealed. They were no longer part of the living world.

They were inside with her, but not trapped. They would not go with her, even if she tried to persuade them, cajole them, order them with all her might. They would not go with her even if they could. A great honour was bestowed on them and they had their own paths to follow. Human life was hard and it was cruel. And it was fleeting. The ancients were more aware of this than most.

In a few hours, she would depart. She would leave the communal area, and ascend the slanting corridor that led to the Queen's Chamber. But for now, they had something she did not, and she stood before them. They each held a carved miniature in their hands.

"My queen," a voice said, followed by several others. The formation of a chorus.

"You are eternity," she said. "And everlastingness."

For them, now, the only possibility was the inevitable. Not even the gods would choose to interfere. The miniatures were coated in fast-acting poison, extracted from apricot kernels, already absorbed by the skin, already entered the bloodstream. She held each of their gazes until the last of them fell to the floor. She left them to their prayers and convulsions.

The time had come to approach the coffin, her mummified husband inside.

She considered his death mask to be only a rough likeness, but given the circumstances, it would have to do. They had shared so much together. She would not say goodbye, because they had said this so many times before. She would not speak of what it was to stare into the eyes of their new-born sons and daughters, because they shared this memory. She could have spoken of a younger man at the festival of Akhet that lasted twenty days, where no man was left standing, except her king, at her side as always. She could have mentioned the king's first wife, Meritites, who had always kept her distance up until her passing. As Queen Henutsen, she may have been his second wife, but always with the knowledge that she was the king's favourite. She was his true love, as much as he was hers. Any additional words on the matter would be inadequate, and all told, best left unsaid.

Except these: "Thank you for a life worth living."

The time was close now; she would enter her chamber and locate the exit secreted at the back. A stone block worked loose and lifted clear. Through this, she would climb into the open, where she would be met by two guards under strict orders to close it behind her. A Pharoah's last wish formed from his last breath. Such were the machinations of fate.

There was one other thing she could say, standing in his presence; a revelation. She owed him that much. There was a name before Henutsen—before the necessity of taking on something more appropriate when securing a place in the royal family. She'd never told a living soul before. Except one, perhaps, who knew already. She would speak it, and this would have to do.

"My name..." she said. A final offering to her one king, her one husband, her one love. This one time, there was no need to whisper. And he, in turn could take this with him all the way to Aaru.

"My name is Evelyn."

*

She steeped a sponge in vinegar then lifted it. It was soaking wet. Gently, carefully, held in the cradle of her hand, determined to keep drippage to a minimum, she was ready to do her work. She liked the small details. They were important to her.

In advance of the first meal of the day, she began to wash her client's feet. Diligently, she removed the dirt from between the toes. She drew concentric circles around the calluses on the soles and heels. As she trimmed the toenails with a knife (dipped in vinegar also), she was aware of snoring coming from above. She prided herself in doing a good job and this was no different. One overzealous snort later, bringing her client with a jolt back to the land of the living, and the transaction was concluded. He paid an adequate amount for the privilege.

Later, she bathed in the fresh water of the Sea of Galilee, keeping a watchful eye in case any passing fishing boat got too close. Later still, while the sun was at its highest point in the sky, she sought out her friends Lily and Tabitha on the Plain.

They were not alone. A large crowd had already gathered to hear the preacher from Nazareth speak.

"Where is the sinful woman? Evie, Evie?" Tabitha asked.

"The one who forgoes love so she may wash men's feet?" Lily said, trying, and failing, not to smirk.

"Okay, okay, stop it," she said with added emphasis, her arms crossed. "You've had your fun."

"Evie, there she is!"

"There you are!"

All three embraced, shrieking with delight, while standing on their tiptoes.

In the distance, the preacher climbed towards the highest point. The three friends continued to chat among themselves.

"There he is."

"Who is he? Is it his first time in Bethsaida?"

"I don't think so. He talks about love and forgiveness. Turning the other cheek. I like that."

"They say he was born in a stable."

"Poor thing."

"You don't hear enough of those types of things, especially from a man. It makes a change for casting eternal damnation for this and that; feeding salt to your donkey."

"He claims he is the son of God."

"Ah then, he's a man after all."

They laughed at this. Evie loved to hear them laugh. It was the sound of freedom.

Tabitha took a look around. "There must be thousands here."

"Is it his birthday, or something?"

"How can you tell?"

"What?"

"Thousands? You gone round and counted every one of them?"

Lily was always a stickler for these kinds of things.

Evie looked around too. Every second or third member of the crowd carried a basket of bread or fish, all bringing food to this one event, for this one man. Such was the charisma of the preacher, she concluded. Such was the devotion he must inspire.

She noticed a familiar face in the crowd, far enough away perhaps not to notice her in return. Although she doubted it.

It was Ammonite, or whatever he was calling himself these days. Dressed in fisherman clothes. He had a full beard, and she was delighted for him. But today wasn't about him.

She could sense a silence was about to descend. She could feel the anticipation bubbling up against each midfoot. A silence so profound it would be heard across the Jordan Valley, across Judea, across the Roman Empire, across the whole wide world itself. Prevailing upon the peasants, farmers, nobility and high priests to prick up their ears. The mothers. The children. Wherever it would take them, and nothing would ever be the same thereafter.

She turned to Tabitha and Lily. "Let's hear what he has to say, and then let's eat," she said.

The preacher reached the summit. As predicted, there fell a collective hush. The preacher opened his arms to acknowledge the multitude and made to speak.

*

It was 1453.

A war correspondent interviewed an army general. Given the time period, one a relatively new type of species and the other a relatively old one.

"General Giustiniani," the war correspondent began, "congratulations on your current assignment and welcome to the great city of Constantinople."

Niceties done with, and conscious of the limited time allocated to him, the war correspondent got straight to the point. "General, do you think that Constantinople will fall?"

The general was dressed in full ceremonial uniform—in full plumage—and man and uniform visibly bristled at the question. He shifted slowly in his seat, causing the medals lining his chest to jingle, seeking to make his irritation known to the cause of the irritation.

The general frowned. "In service of the city named after Constantine the Great, the Emperor who brought Christianity to the Roman Empire? There is no greater honour," he said. It could be said he answered a question, just not the one put to him. Another question: "Remind me again, do you have a name?"

The war correspondent took pause, allowed himself a secret sigh, resigned to an interviewee of a mind to be difficult. The general demanded indulgence, so he indulged him. "My name is Adam Froissart."

"Ah, of course you are. And your credentials?"

The general wore so many feathers, the war correspondent had to fight the urge to sneeze. "I have been to England, Scotland, Italy and the Low Countries, and all the battlefields between. I was there at the end of the Hundred Years' War. I reported from the field when the French drove back the English at the siege of Orléans. I was at the trial of Joan of Arc."

"You hardly seem old enough," the general said.

"Trust me, General, I'm older than I look."

"A reporter on the field, eh? No stranger to wading through mud, shit and blood? The spoils of war?"

At this, the general gave himself a resounding slap on the thigh. He wasn't one to sit still.

"No stranger, General. Of course, nor are you. Your reputation in Genoa precedes you. And here we are, the emperor appoints the great General Giustiniani as Commander in Chief in defence of none other than the great capital. Although, the army that arrived with you—700 strong I believe—consists mainly of mercenaries for hire, does it not? When not fighting, there are reports throughout the city of bar brawls, the harassing of gentiles…"

"There is much to be said of a Christian name." The general tapped several fingers on his chin. "There is an element of choice not afforded by a surname. Were you named after your father? A favourite uncle? Perhaps something biblical.

"Adam, I like the name.

"A-dam.

"In answer to your question, Adam Froissart, Constantinople will not fall."

"Even though it is widely held," the war correspondent pressed, "that the Sultan's army outnumbers those enlisted in the city garrison seven to one?"

"My devotion to Genoa is matched only by my commitment to Constantinople. The city cannot fall. Sultan Mehmed's forces will not breach the city's famed defences."

An air of serenity befell the general as he uttered the words: "Nothing can scale the Theodosian Walls. This is my pledge as a general of the Byzantine Empire."

The war correspondent wrote all of this down in his abbreviated scrawl. Upon completion, he leaned forward and made to speak, but in anticipation of this, General Giustiniani shot up a hand, strangling at birth any words to spring from the interviewer's mouth. "My dear Adam, in a thousand years there will still be a Byzantine Empire. No one will remember there ever was an Ottoman Empire.

"The Constantine line will go on live forever. The world will never know another."

"Ah huh." The war correspondent nodded while writing this down as well. The general's good humour aside, the city of Constantinople had been under siege for the best part of fifty days. As the city shook and trembled around them, it seemed incongruous to talk of the permanence of an imperial dynasty. But he had it down in writing.

And yet for now, he had to be selective—to be careful of what he reported and did not report. This wasn't the time to tell the full story. Such a thing would only serve to open himself up to reprisals from the powers that be, or those wishing to curry favour from such. That, and he would no longer have access to the major players, at least this side of the perennial conflict. To tell a true picture, warts and all, that would have to wait.

For now, he had his soundbite.

"In a thousand years there will still be a Byzantine Empire!" so the city callers bellowed, clanging their bells as they went about the business of spreading the news courtesy of war correspondent Adam Froissart.

It was right that he was here. Constantinople was the gateway between two great continents and the empire builders of Europe and Asia. But in these uncertain times of burgeoning ideologies, the importance of Constantinople had become a curse. The city was the central point in a battle for dominance between Orthodox Roman Catholic Byzantine to the west and Muslim Ottoman to the east. Controlled by the former and coveted by the latter, leading to siege after siege. A vicious circle, gears on gears, older than Methuselah, spanning centuries, a scar on the modern world to come. Where else could the war correspondent be but here?

A day after their first encounter, Adam Froissart answered the general's call to join him at the Wall. He wiped the hair from his eyes, courtesy of an unruly fringe, so he could properly lay eyes on it. Four miles long, fifty feet tall, sixteen feet thick. A giant monolith of towers, gates and stone. Grey wall, grey sky. Grey filled the senses. Its vastness only equalled by its permanence. The wall had stood for a thousand years.

Beyond the wall was the Bosporus. The waterway and its ports lent the city much of its strategic significance. It also brought danger. The unwanted attention of a naval fleet of a foreign power.

The city within was a series of walled villages. Palaces sat next to slum tenements. Civilians going about their business with heads bowed; the weight of rationing, subsistence and fear bearing down on them, preventing them from looking up at the sunlight or staring at the moon. It didn't matter who you spoke to, no one wanted war but it came to them in perpetuity.

And now the city was in a state of suspended animation. It seemed to Adam that at that precise time the only movement to be had was coming from the mouth of Giustiniani. He wore a uniform similar to the day before but with fewer feathers and more medals.

"I am disturbed," he said.

"You are, general? How so?"

"Rumours persist that our defences will not hold. Words—damnable treason. They are designed to obfuscate the obvious and inevitable."

"Which is?"

"Victory."

The war correspondent considered questioning the assertion, but as if reading his mind, the general puffed out his chest. Words of dissent were left desiccated and dried out in the war correspondent's mouth.

It was the general who spoke next. "The Venetians are coming!" There followed raucous laughter from him, placing a gauntleted hand on the war correspondent's shoulder. "The Venetian Senate is to send 800 troops and 15 galleys to the capital! They will be here in a matter of weeks! Salvation is at hand!"

The reporter smiled thinly in return. One thousand years, a matter of weeks, the war correspondent was compelled to look beyond the white noise. To contemplate the now. The reality of the siege, the casualties ensued, meant the line defending the city was spread too thin. And even here, even now, there was an overreliance on a ragtag mercenary army.

He stared at the wall again. The legacy of every barrage that had come before. Four miles of debris, pieces of broken grey, the once great wall crumbling before his eyes. The weight of history falling on his shoulders (now the general had withdrawn his hand). The population of Constantinople in the 12th century at its peak was half a million, now reduced three centuries on, to a meagre 50,000.

It all smacked of one thing, but not of victory or salvation. "Everything has been leading to this," the war correspondent whispered, so quiet, little more than mouthing the words. "A last stand."

The Ottoman fleet had already taken control of the Bosporus. It controlled the waters surrounding the city. The Ottoman strategy was clear; take the city before the arrival of reinforcements.

He was still staring, still contemplative, as the current military barrage punched a hole through the wall.

There was an almighty sound. Borne of shuddering, inescapable movement. One would be forgiven for believing the world had fallen off its axis. And then...

An unnatural silence, as if the noise around the war correspondent was too big for him to comprehend. Surrounding him like a seiche, swimming at the bottom of a river, struggling for air. Not quite ready to climb on shore. Fins instead of legs.

The general shouted orders, darting to and fro, a human boomerang rallying his forces. But such was the magnitude of surrounding events, the scale of it, anything he could muster seemed so tiny, so oddly hopeless.

The silence had to mean something. A frontal infantry assault soon followed, breaching the city gates. It was the end game three centuries in the making. It would be over in hours.

The war correspondent dropped to one knee, exposed, encircled by outbreaks of hand-to-hand combat. The flash of steel. The sound of gunpowder. Thrashing limbs, hellbent on the destruction of the other. The ground sticky with blood. The swallowing of bile. The stench of shit and sweat.

The general was still close to him, as if connected by an invisible elastic band, but it was the war correspondent who saw it first. Originating from one of the towers, a glint of metal against the grey. The swooping of a golden eagle.

A crossbow bolt punctured the general's shoulder. The downward trajectory established by the bolt did not stop there, throwing the general to the ground.

The general, hardly moving, was shouting, incoherent. Soldiers gathered around him. They dragged him from the frontline.

The war correspondent's close proximity proved his undoing. Such was the chaos around him, he was pushed to the ground by a friendly hand. Such was the extent of the melee he was kicked in the head by a friendly boot.

Couldn't get up even if he tried. A haziness, a dismantling of the senses, washing over him. Nothing moving in real time. All like a dream. Even more so, now he was losing consciousness. Undone. Unravelled. The general was undermined by undiluted overconfidence. A sense of entitlement. The war correspondent was along for the ride.

The city behind them, in front of them family units huddled together in their homes. The wall cast a different type of shadow now. Without its protection where would they be? What will happen when—

Lights out.

Later—it had to happen at some point—Adam Froissart opened his eyes. He'd been here before, although his current surroundings were unfamiliar to him, except for the face that peered down at him.

"Evelyn," he said.

"Well, well," she said. "You talk in your sleep, Adam. Adam…

"When did you ditch the name Ammonite?"

He moved his hand to the back of his head, reassured it was still there. "When it became unfashionable to share a name with those 13th Century rabble-rousers the *Sons of Ammon*, or the name of a cephalopod fossil for that matter."

He sat up from the makeshift bedding, woozy. His hand shifted and flitted around his head dressing, recently acquired. "You patched me up. Thank you. "Where did you find me? How did you find me?

"Where are we?" All around was dark and cavernous. He noticed a wine cellar adjoining the other side of the room. Too much dust, long undisturbed, to read the labels on the bottles.

"So many questions," she said, smiling through the darkness. "But I suppose it's the nature of what you do. You're a reporter. It's not difficult to keep tabs. I pay a retainer to some of the general's soldiers. They brought you here in your time of need.

"I was already a person of independent means before I came to the capital. I married a nobleman approaching his dotage and on the lookout for a fourth wife. A marriage of convenience, you might choose to call it. When he passed, no one questioned my various business interests. I have a penchant for acquiring property with cellars and underground rooms. There are other strays hiding out in other places. A network of safe havens from the invading hoard. It's not much. It's not enough. They are the lucky ones. I can't offer shelter to a whole city. And here we are."

"Underground," he said, taking a moment for his present reality to sink in. "And the city?"

"The general is gone, his forces dispersed, a vacuum filled by Mehmed's army. Above us is the final assault. There will be a period of looting. The ransacking of the Orthodox churches. People will die. They'll be taken as slaves.

"While we wait it out underground. Waiting for the transition from one world order to the next."

"You welcome a Muslim state?"

"I just want it to stop. For it to wear itself out. The murder, the insanity."

The colour drained from her face. At this moment she looked her true age, as ancient as the fault lines that trace the earth. She could make a difference, but she was still only one person. "Whoever controls Constantinople won't change where it is. Or what it is. A foothold in the Mediterranean; access to the Black Sea. They'll probably take a leaf out of your book though, Adam, and call the city by another name."

She looked away, shaking, faltering. "I don't want to be that person who tells such things. I don't want these things to turn out true." She gathered herself, then touched the side of her face, stronger than she had ever been. "Families will be given the chance to buy back the freedom of their loved ones," she said. At least for a little while.

"The price I suppose, rarely worth paying, of having a place in history."

He straightened his back and rolled his shoulders. "We'll see it out together," he said.

She blinked at this. Made a scrunched-up face. "Oh no, Adam Froissart, some strays can't be kept. They have to be set free."

They waited until dark to emerge and sneak through the city. It was an arid night. The streets were eerily quiet. The cobblestones under their feet were wet and slippy in places, but they did not hang around to find out why. There was the odd scream to emanate from the darkness; some muffled crying that followed them from one back alley to the next. Otherwise, the silence was deafening.

Evelyn led the way to a building behind a wall; one far smaller in scale than the wall of before. But where the first wall was designed to protect a city, this one shielded a stable.

She motioned towards his head. "Keep the bandage on and they'll think you're no kind of threat. For now, the occupying forces are more concerned with those trying to enter the city from the West, rather than the people looking to flee it."

They entered the stable and stood in front of a grey horse. She stroked its main and whispered words from an ancient language in its ear.

She turned her attention back to Adam. "Take the horse. This is for you."

He stood still; couldn't move a muscle even if he wanted to. "You ran from me at the beginning," he said, "When I was knee-deep in the primordial ooze. "Near or far, one part of the world or the other, I always sensed you were out there. And now I've caught up with you, you save me again."

Instinctively, they hugged. His grip was tighter than hers.

"Come with me," he said.

But as soon as they'd come together, something was pushing them back.

"No," she said, slowly shaking her head. "There are darker times ahead. Centuries of bloodshed and fore-boding and atrocity. You feel it too. We can't escape it. Together we remind each other of this fact. It is too oppressive. We can't be with each other."

"Then, when?"

Her hands danced. She hunched her shoulders. "I have my other strays, remember. And this is my home. While you—

"You have a story to tell."

He mounted the horse, her parting gift to him. Still, he could not resist holding out his hand to her one final time. "And you?"

She took three quick breaths. "I am used to change. Times of great upheaval. I was there at the birth of Christianity. You were there as well. One of the five thousand at Bethsaida. I saw you in the crowd. Did you see me?"

"I'm not…" It was the turn of Adam Froissart to shake his head, more wearily even than Evelyn had before. At last, the realisation from him that this latest encounter had come to an end. He nodded and rode off. Never to look back.

He rode on, passing on the way hundreds of refugees, carrying on their backs what remained of their possessions. A skewered procession, a ragged diaspora. He did not stop to offer help or encouragement. They were on their path and the war correspondent was on his.

The horse got him as far as the crossing into Greece, where he traded it for passage to Austria. On reaching the Austrian border, word had spread of the war correspondent's journey, and he was able to secure a sponsor who funded the last leg of his trip to Mainz, Germany and—

His sponsor was Johannes Gutenberg, who had a long beard only matched by the length of his cloak. Johannes Gutenberg had dried ink on his hands.

The war correspondent's journey was at an end, and Gutenberg was there to hold a door open to him. "I believe you have a story to tell," he said to him.

Beyond the door, lying in wait for them, was a standing mechanism which dominated the room; three feet wide and as long and as tall as a man. A device that took a composite of metal letters and applied pressure to a surface of ink.

Exhausted after his journey, still recovering from his injuries, but in the grip of something greater, Adam Froissart could not rest, not right now. His story was his journey, and to tell it, he had to be detached. He had to look on, separate from humanity, gathering information, having talked to combatants. The note-taking during the ferocity of battle; he wrote down what mattered. The accounts of those he'd left behind.

The facts at his fingertips, warts and all, but where to begin? Warring philosophies? The weaponizing of religion? Hell as a battleground?

There was the mud, shit and blood, of course. But there was more to it than that. Something fundamental. Where was the glory in three centuries of war? What did it say about the human condition? That there was a part of humanity that indulged in self-sabotage, a desire to keep itself from evolving into something better. Merely to repeat. And in the end, who will judge humanity if it can't judge itself? Will it fall to God almighty? Or something less prosaic and more elemental? Judged by the earth they walk upon. The ellipsoid of living organisms they call home.

He would ask the question in the hope that others may ask it also. Question it and dare to imagine the opposite. Centuries of war had created hell on earth, and its name was Constantinople.

Once he had relied on criers around cities, around towns, around streets to spread the word. The arrival of the mechanical Gutenberg press, set up before him, was about to usher in a renaissance. The era of mass communication, and with it the modern world.

Situated next to the press was a desk. On top of the desk was a quill and ink and paper. The war correspondent sat down to it, very much aware that the printing press beside him needed feeding.

The second voice in the room informed him in passing of the death of Emperor Constantine XI.

It was the end of Rome. It was the rise of the Ottoman Empire. Everything changes. Everything stays the same. The rise and fall, and maybe rise again of Constantinople.

Head down, quill in hand, "Danke schön," the war correspondent said. And with this, he began.

*

The sound of battle abated, signalling much-needed respite for the 72nd General Hospital Unit.

One of the medics, a graduate from Kalamazoo, Michigan, who went by the name of Adam Johnson, took the chance to have a smoke outside the mess hall. He smoked with his left hand.

He looked down to discover that he absentmindedly held a scalpel in his right. He rarely held anything else these days.

The Unit was based at a disused fairground outside of Naples. Most of the rides had been removed except for the stripped-down carousel that occupied the courtyard.

Many of the main buildings were renovated to accommodate the main office: the billets, bakery, kitchen, wards and operating theatres.

HQ looked down on operations. Thrown in for good measure was a mural of Benito Mussolini, now riddled with bullet holes.

The war was never far, and where there was strafing and shelling, there would be stray bombs and shells. Evidence of bomb damage was everywhere, necessitating around the complex a myriad of makeshift repairs consisting of plexiglass and tarmacadam. By way of consolation, albeit a scant one, the battlefront had moved north but such notions of reprieve would inevitably prove as arbitrary as temporary.

It was winter, or as close as, but even so unseasonably cold. So cold, Adam Johnson could not distinguish the smoke of his cigarette from his frozen breath. He slid the scalpel into his pocket. Smoke finished, he clasped his hands together and held them close to his chest. He did this before reluctantly entering the mess hall.

He joined the queue to the canteen. While he waited, he kept his gaze fixed on his feet. It was then that he noticed his left hand holding his right wrist. Another medic joined the queue, whistling sharply between clenched teeth and standing directly behind him.

Adam was not a rebel, not a leader, he did not want any trouble. He was just so tired, and weary, so he did the right thing; he kept his head down. He willed his hand to be steady. He stepped aside and gave up his place in the queue.

All around the canteen, he was aware of bouts of coughing playing catch across the hall. If he closed his eyes, he could imagine it as stray shells one landing after another.

After lunch, he visited one of his patients in the recovery ward. A soldier admitted with internal bleeding around the abdominal area. Operating, Adam had staunched the bleeding to the point the patient was no longer critical but had a fever.

Sometimes they would receive POWs to treat: Italians and Germans. And sometimes Adam would visit them, too. They would stare at him with a hatred so intense he feared for his own safety. The harsh reality was that it was no different with some of his own troops, take this latest patient for example. If he would look at him at all.

It was the longest day, but even days such as this must come to an end.

With this, he closed his eyes.

Get some rest. It would begin all again tomorrow. Lifting his right hand, willing it to sleep. His breath in tatters, a faint echo of the coughing bouncing through the billet and wards. That, and the occasional death rattle.

In the morning, respiratory illness and infection had taken root through both staff and patients, spreading like wildfire, reducing the number of personnel to that of a skeleton staff. Such a turn of events could never be regarded as anything good, but even so, this was terrible timing. The front had drifted south again.

It was always the front. The weight of it on all of their shoulders.

In the days that followed, the casualties began to pile up at the 72nd Unit, literally. A broken regiment from the US Seventh Army arrived by the trainload. This amounted to hundreds of wounded, walking and otherwise, they had to make room for.

Putting up tents in the courtyard. Converting a chunk of HQ into a makeshift ward.

Another freight train, signifying even more casualties to come. The latest arrivals were placed in the attics of buildings.

Medic Adam Johnson was assigned to one such area above the main barracks. Climbing the attic ladder, he was joined by a military nurse and two ambulatory patients having been pressed into service. The nurse wore a dark blue cloak over an off-white uniform. The patients carried with them a mop each.

Below, beds piled high, in barracks already riddled with infection. Above, over thirty wounded, some screaming and writhing in agony, while others were mercifully unconscious. But merciful to whom?

Medic and support team faced each other, faces taut, grim, making the mental leap, about to spur into action. To transit through the wounded. Medic, assisted by the nurse, to stabilise, staunch and repair. The ambulatory patients to mop up blood and fluid, to try and prevent seepage from leaking through the attic floor.

The nurse placed her hand on Adam's shoulder. She used the position of leverage to lean forward and whisper in the medic's ear.

"Remember our orders," she said. "Whites first, your kind second."

Sewing up wounds, sawing off limbs, operating at a rudimentary level, stopping the bleeding. Washing hands in petroleum-based disinfectant which burned away a layer of epidermis from his hands. He wasn't a rebel, wasn't a leader. He didn't want a court martial. Everything was a blur. Needing to localise, only focus on the body parts requiring attention. Seeing double, two hands shifting, with needle and thread. His head shook, and by osmosis, this kept his hands steady.

Odours of ragged sheets and creeping rigor mortis. Tapping of the veins. Urgent pleas, garbled requests, for absentee friends and family. The past moving effortlessly amongst the present.

Administering morphine. Brutal surgery. A revolving door. The flow was relentless. Triage? There was no triage. All required urgent attention. The fatally wounded were left to be consumed by their shrinking mortality.

Moving from one bed, barely a mattress and little more, to another. He was an automaton. A golem. A bag of gristle and liquid and muscle memory.

Shapes into shapes. Following orders, body caked in sweat, blindsided, a creature of instinct but nothing else.

"This is no one." At last, he found the air in his lungs. Mouth moving, trembling, he found himself saying something. Sinew coming apart in his hands. "This is everyone."

It was a long day. The longest day. Eventually, he was relieved of duty and was able to step down the ladder, taking care not to trip and fall on the way.

He was exhausted. Beyond exhaustion. The world was at war, and not for the first time. What was it worth? The colour of its skin? The world was so tiny around him. And sick and forlorn and dying. The world was the 72nd General Hospital Unit.

That night, the longest night, subjugated by ragged breath, the sure knowledge that something was broken inside. But that did not mean there would be no tomorrow. It was there if he looked hard enough. But it was the dead of night, the dead of night, the dead of night. He lifted his right hand from the bedcover and watched it shake.

For now, waiting for his hand to stop so the rest of him could try and follow suit.

*

"The White House is aware of reports to the contrary, but there is little credence to the idea all this will go away with the onset of the warm weather."

The contrary. He tightened the knot of his tie, making it a little too tight around his neck for comfort. That was the way he liked it.

"It is unlikely this new virus is going to go away anytime soon."

Anytime soon. He grabbed the remote and with a tut,

louder than it should have been, he switched off the TV. He had no idea why the darn thing was switched on in the first place. All he wanted was peace and quiet.

But the moment had passed. He stared at the now dormant screen. "Since when did we start working for the government?" he said.

He grabbed his jacket.

He lived in a sixth-floor apartment on The Montague, and the whole point of a sixth-floor apartment on The Montague was to make you think you didn't live on the sixth floor of anywhere. The walls were recent recipients of a fresh lick of paint, making the interiors seem even more self-contained. A capsule. It was it and him.

He left the apartment.

He was down at ground level.

He could have chosen tens of other restaurants, all only a few blocks away, but the one he set his mind to was Textbook. There was no ulterior motive behind this, just the desire to prove that he didn't care which one. To himself, to whoever. Not about this and not about anything.

He nudged forward, shoulder first, into a bracing wind. Three quick steps, then a slower one, then three quick steps again. To show he was in control. To go where he wanted to go, but not too fast and not too slow.

The streets were much quieter than usual. Even the ghosts had taken the day off. He decided to take advantage of the space opened up to him by taking a more circuitous route. He felt impulsive, impish even. He wanted to hug and shake the hand of the next person who passed him. He'd say, *look at me, I survived the Antonine Plague, The Black Death, a multitude of cholera and flu pandemics. I was there when AIDS happened, for Chrissakes.*

It would be a long handshake. It would probably get quite intense where the other person was concerned. In the current environment, who wanted a further reminder of what was happening in the world? The more he thought of such unintended consequences, the more he talked himself out of the idea.

He walked past the Brooklyn Hospital Centre. The concourse spread out before him, but away from the main doors, under the cover of low light, he spied several orderlies in masks lifting shadowy shapes into the back of a truck.

On the side of the truck was a print of a rolled rug being flattened. There was the name of a carpet store, one he didn't recognise. He could have stopped to take a closer look but this would have brought with it the risk of drawing attention to himself, and no one wanted that.

He'd lived through such hysteria many times before, verging on becoming something of a bad joke. If he couldn't prove it to anyone else, because there was no one else around, then he could at least prove it to himself.

He'd survived every human plague that had come before. He'd survived war. Except for the fact he hadn't survived any of it, strictly speaking. No plagues or pandemics or world wars. He'd lived through them, the more accurate description.

He took a moment outside Textbook to put on a mask. Diner policy dictated he wouldn't be seen to a table without one. He hoped the mushroom omelette he intended to order would be worth it.

As he entered and waited at the front desk, he noticed a flat screen fixed to the side wall. Up on the screen was a familiar face. A depressingly familiar face. The sound was turned down but he could make out the words. Make out enough of them.

"At this point, the risk of infection is low, but this could change. We ask everyone to be vigilant. To be alert. Wear a mask to protect you and those around you from the spread."

To be alert. On her approach, the hostess glanced at the TV. Then, facing front, she read the obvious distaste on his face. She flashed him a tight smile.

She bent down at the knees behind the front desk and rummaged around the lower section, eventually coming up for air. Remote in hand, she switched channels to a football game which miraculously was being played to a full crowd. The game going ahead made possible by Presidential endorsement, contrary to the advice issued by his own taskforce. A box of contradiction bundled up as a miracle.

"Not what you want to be seeing on a night like this," the hostess said, tossing the remote back where it came from.

"Not on any night, if you ask me," he said, face relaxing.

He was brought a glass of water, only to wave a hand and ask for it to be taken away. Ordered a beer. He was brought his meal and he dutifully took off the mask. Squirrelled it away in the front pocket of his jeans.

He sat back and made several slices through the omelette, scraping the plate as he did so. He was eating alone, but this didn't detract from the communal nature of the experience. Around him, couples and small groups talked, ate, and drank. The formation of delimited jerky bubbles around each table, positioned a foot or so apart. Everyone was calm, everyone was safe, so long as they were masticating or digesting.

A man a couple of tables from him stood up quickly. His face turned an unnatural red. The colour of fake blood.

His whole body was in spasm. He was coughing. Uncontrollable heaving.

Others around the man reacted, they stood as well, backs slightly bent, closed body language. Instinctively they shied away from the coughing man. Like he was the centre of a maelstrom.

The thought of safety now shattered; the way those around him reacted, the man could have had a gun in his hand, or a knife. But he had a cough, which was more than enough, and people were already starting to leave the restaurant.

A man with an omelette was standing too, but otherwise going against the flow.

He approached the coughing man, holding up an open hand; wanting to help. He grabbed the man by the shoulders. Turned him around so his back was against him. Wracked by pain, an internal force, compliant, folding in on itself.

He slammed an open palm between the man's shoulder blades. He did it again, several times.

The man's body remained contorted, the back of his neck an unnatural puce, but there was no accompanying noise. There was shape to his movement now. A blunt edge. Non-serrated, at least on the outside.

He placed his arms around the man's midriff and pulled him towards him, lifting his diaphragm; air expelled from the lungs.

A projectile of half-chewed steak, frayed at the edges, launched like a cannonball from the man's airway.

He released the man, who fell to his knees, falling clear of a chair. His hands were moving, scrabbling around the restaurant's wooden floor, needing to do something, anything. A proof of life.

He looked around. From the opposite side of the room, the hostess took one step forward.

"Dear god," she said, "Heimlich manoeuvre."

"Don't think," he said, casting a glance at the chunk of killer steak—which was propelled across the restaurant before ending up firmly stuck on the far wall, barely chewed, given a glossy finish from a combination of digestive juice and dark saliva—and then back at his meal, "it's called that anymore."

The omelette wasn't worth it, he decided.

That night, he lay down on his bed. Not feeling

great. Not feeling invulnerable. He put his phone down on the side cabinet, lay back down, and stretched out his arm to make sure that the phone was still in reach from his current position. After the day he had, he needed that kind of reassurance.

His head was swollen, temples closing in against the other.

Jumbled, random thoughts. Of testing and Paxlovid. Closing the border to China. Mount Rushmore fireworks display. Wear a mask. Don't wear a mask. Keep your distance. Don't keep your distance. Ring-a-ring o' roses. Wet markets. Lab leaks. The fat is in the fire. Vials of hydroxychloroquine were held in an underground bunker somewhere.

He counted the beads of sweat one by one on his brow and then slipped into dream. He was back in the plains. They were Hominin again.

"Ammonite," she said.

"Evelyn," he said. "I thought you were close, but I couldn't be sure. Maybe, there will come a day we'll stay in one place long enough to have a proper conversation."

"Maybe," she was nodding. "Yes, one day, when it's time. When we don't have any other choice."

"I will always have a choice," he said chest puffed out.

"We owe the world so much," she said, "we owe the world so little. We mingle. We build relationships—sometimes. We help shape things, and maybe as way of an added bonus we learn from this. And then we reset." She made to sneeze, stopped herself, and then smiled. "We come and go like the children's nursery rhyme.

"A-tishoo!" she said.

He woke in the morning, if you could call it waking, both unbearably hot and cold. He couldn't taste his spit.

He reached for his phone and the exertion knocked the wind out of him. There was an enduring pain in his joints, in his knuckles. He took his phone and texted out a message to his boss. He could hardly see what was in front of him. At the mercy of predictive text.

Text sent, he placed his hand on his chest, which was hot. Hotter than the surface of the sun. Hotter than the asteroid that plummeted to earth, burning up in the atmosphere with the sole intention of wiping out giant reptiles.

He lay his head back on the pillow, but the way the world was shifting underneath him, jostling him up and down and across, like he was on a rollercoaster on full tilt, he knew he couldn't stay there long.

Needed to get up. Somehow tear himself away.

He had medical insurance came with the job. And he was never going to argue against it or say he didn't need it. Didn't want to come across as some kind of madman.

The coughing began on the walk to the centre. He had put on as many layers as he could endure, including a scarf he used to wrap around his mouth. He'd foregone the tie, even though he could feel it tighten around his neck.

Each cough brought an explosion in his chest. A mini-execution. He began to count frantically, between coughs, furiously trying to take his mind off the pain, while unable to focus on anything else.

1,2,3,4...cough

1,2,3...cough

1,2...cough

Until even something as simple as counting from one became a redundant exercise.

He was woken from his pain-drenched reverie when asked for a name. Ammonite? Froissart? Johnson? No, it wasn't that. Blinking. Too much fog. He struggled to remember.

"Adam Moss." Having checked his wallet, the hospital attendant answered his own question.

"No relation to Elisabeth or Kate," he mumbled.

"What?" The hospital attendant fired him a quizzical look.

"I sometimes get asked that."

He kept his head down after this. He was seated in a room, kept away from other patients, clutching the front of his jacket. Twist.

"Can't…" he said, barely struggling to get a single word out.

He sat in front of a small television. Apart from him and that, there was nothing else in the room. There was nothing else to see.

And there she was, occupying as much as the dimensions of the screen allowed.

"There's nothing to say, some baseless anecdotes apart, that we now have a shortage of beds and a shortage of ventilators. We're not there yet, there's no hard fast evidence we're close to this."

"Can't…"

He was down on the floor on his side. His hand still twisting the woven material in his hand. His chest was on fire. His mouth was a wet ring that formed a sodden imprint on the scarf covering it. Such a simple thing to take for granted. He could not breathe.

The scarf was stripped away and replaced by clear plastic.

Another dream. A lurid one. The Roman Army, swathed in red, returning home victorious from Mesopotamia. It is 165 years before the birth of Christ. Unwittingly, they brought something back with them, inside them, something microscopic, lying in wait, but not for long. An eruption. The Roman army in full armour, shields and swords, falling one by one like dominoes. Skin blistering. Changing the colour of their piss. Taking their last breaths, writing out their names with their fingers on the dirt for fear otherwise they'd be forgotten. It ripped a hole through them. For this was something that could do to the Roman Army what opposing armies could not. They named it the Antonine Plague.

It was like yesterday, this long time ago. A tiny voice:

I don't want to die. I cannot die.

Tinier still:

Ring-a-ring o' roses,
A pocket full of posies.
A-tishoo! A-tishoo!

Random:

Physician, heal thyself.

Except that he wasn't a doctor anymore—or a war correspondent, or a fisherman. He worked in realty.

This is it. I'm gonna die.

He came to in a hospital bed. Floating in negative airflow. Shredded nerves like porcupine quills. Borrowed oxygen leaked out of every pore of his skin.

A masked doctor leaned over him, wearing a dazzlingly white uniform, and looking every inch the Lone Ranger.

"Got you to ICU in the proverbial nick of time," the doctor said. "For a while there, things were a little sticky…"

Even though he couldn't see it, he could hear it, the inner smile in the doctor's voice. The doctor wasn't finished there, producing an iPad from what seemed like thin air. He lifted a finger, theatrically pressing it against the screen. "…But you're well on the way to recovery.

"Mm-hmm, well on the way."

"Thanks, doc," he said, his voice deep and croaky, plummeting the depths, such was his embattled chest.

His embittered lungs.

His many lives.

In response, or so it came across that way, the doctor checked his watch. "Now, what to eat to fortify recovery, I'd say 100 grams of protein. Say, nut butter, cheese, poultry…"

Now his eyes were accustomed to the light, he noticed over the doctor's shoulder, another screen fixed to another wall.

There she was predictably enough in her White House role as advisor. Timeless, never to tell people what they wanted to hear, but what they needed to hear.

"...Milk."

"Think hard," she said, "about non-essential activities like professional haircuts. And firework displays."

"...Yoghurt, fish, protein shakes."

The man called Adam Moss drew strength from somewhere, not necessarily a good place. "We've been here before. Shut up. Over and over again," he said. Kicking up a fuss along with the bedsheets. "Shut the fuck up!"

Bringing the focus back to doctor and patient. The former, underneath the mask, reacted to the latter's outburst with a sympathetic smile. But when it came down to it, more preoccupied by thoughts of sleep, or of his own mortality. The reality was, among the coughing and wheezing and the patient's obvious displeasure at being alive, which he assumed was temporary, that the doctor could barely make out a single word.

We all fall down!

*

"Hold me."

That's what they said, the last thing they said, at least on the outside. She leaned forward and respected their wishes, even though she was terrified she'd apply too much force when holding them, causing their chest, which was already fragile, to cave in.

Except that the nodules around their body and the nanites which patrolled their bloodstream wouldn't allow such a thing to happen. Wouldn't allow matters to get so brittle.

Accumulation and decumulation in equal measure. Through the ages, her body had tired of the appendix and dispensed with the need for wisdom teeth. The coccyx, the pyramidalis muscle, the spleen—all surplus to requirements.

She had acquired a number of implants along the way. Augmented retinas that allowed her to see in the dark. A restoration clip that cut down the time she needed to sleep. A mucus inhibitor.

They had none of those things. Had eschewed it all. There was nothing to be done that could have prolonged their existence. Nothing palatable. The insertion of foreign bodies, no matter how benign, was not an option. They had changed enough already. Shorter chromosomes equalled shorter lifespans. That was it. This is what it transpired to.

And so, she sat by their bedside and contemplated her life against theirs. The vastness that separated them. The stretching of existence on one hand, and its contraction on the other.

With a soft buzz, which sent a ripple through her cortex, her internal calendar informing her of her ten o'clock. With a kiss to their forehead, she took her leave of the hospice environs. Her head was full of inescapable thoughts. The imminent death of one's clone was a complicated business.

Her ten o'clock was already waiting for her in the family room.

"Madam President," she said.

The President was dressed in light cream and light blue. The colours of healing. Her face was gaunt, her eyelids heavy.

"I came as soon as I heard," the President said. "I am so sorry. Is there any way I can help?"

She shook her head. There was nothing to do but wait.

"Eve, is there hope?"

"There is always hope, Madam President."

"But in this case…?"

Not that it needed repeating, but she could have reminded her that it was made clear at the outset that the cloning program was a long shot. They had to do something, even if this proved to be nothing more than symbolic as if a demonstration of not giving up would somehow be enough. But that was never going to be enough.

This was the Age of Miracles, which was the Age of Fusion. Humanity had solved many of its problems, only for it to be caught out by a twist of fate.

Of fate and destiny.

Of impending extinction.

A viper in the grass.

They hoped for a better outcome.

She had walked the earth for 370 million years. In the beginning, she was an evolved lungfish, set subsequently to live out countless lives. A pebble skipping on the water's surface. They'd hoped her clone would shed some light on the situation. But her clone was no different to any other. Lifespan of thirty to thirty-five years, without enhancements. A stone that sank on the first bounce.

In terms of the current conversation, that this all should remain unsaid was a kindness.

"How can it be?" the President asked. "Analytics say I'll live to 176, but what kind of life is it to live in a sterile world?"

She reached out and patted the President on the shoulder. A pointless act on her part, clumsy, instantly regretting it, but not bitterly. "There is nothing to link the two phenomena," she said.

"Oh? Nothing scientific." A smile from the President, which was unexpected. She pointed at her midriff. "Except what's in the gut."

They stood one to the other, mirroring a type of stoicism. One masking her disappointment, the other her disillusionment.

"Madam President."

"Eve."

She returned to the hospice. She returned to them. Lying deathly still. As if they had already passed into the cloned version of an afterlife. What she would give for even a twitch.

Before they lapsed, when fit and healthy, they would meet up once or twice a year. They'd go to the park, a different one each time if they could. They'd follow this ritual, a playful one, where they would search for the ideal spot.

The one they were looking for had to be a good height. Two sets of sturdy branches forming two paths, separate and clear, but close enough for them to hear the other talk. With this in mind, they would evaluate the trees.

Once satisfied, they would climb. And as they climbed, they caught up.

"What's up?" she would ask usually.

"Nothing much," they answered. "I think one of my wisdom teeth is pushing through. On the left side. I took a Panadol."

"On the…?"

She gave her head a little shake. It didn't seem right to reminisce while their body lay in such a way. So dormant. External life all but extinguished. She looked down and contemplated being that close to knowing mortality. She wanted to be with them any way she can. Dutifully, delicately, she peeled a nodule from their temple.

She climbed into the hospice bed and lay down on her side. Her arm formed an arch as she placed the nodule, which was still warm, just above her ear.

She was inside their head. She accessed the relevant memory.

She stepped into it.

Taking hold of a bough pendulous above her. Pulling herself up; keep going.

"On the left side?" she said. "Seriously?"

"Seriously. Why would anyone joke about something like toothache?"

"Good point. It's just…" She flexed her jaw. The left-hand side. "…I thought I was done with those."

They stopped climbing, tried to find a reasonable balance while assuming as horizontal a position as possible. Their hand close to the side of their face. As close as the fingertips. They caught her gaze from several feet away, and they held it.

"It's a little sore," they said. "I didn't realise how much I clenched my teeth, until now. I promise myself a hundred times a day I'll stop doing it. There's a part of my brain that struggles to keep up, I think it's kind of wonderful."

"Of course," she said, looking away, continuing to climb. "Can't imagine why I said that." She wanted to put some space between her and them, a crude attempt to alleviate her embarrassment. "Funny reaction."

They looked up at an angle and saw an identical shape, the same muscular arms, the same sized feet. The same voice batted back at them, even with the vaping. But it was not difficult for them to think of themselves as their own person, not when one was forever while the other's life was as fleeting as a hummingbird.

Still, there was no bitterness, they always knew what they were. It was never kept from them. And what does bitterness get you in any case, except the waste of precious time.

"I'm my own person," they said, but not to her.

And she had climbed so far above her, anyway. She was unsure if she'd made the right choice of memory. Sure, a conversation to think back on, to dwell on, but not right now. No looking back, please, no time for regrets. Not over a tooth. A feeling, a pull, caused her to look up and realise white light was occupying the space where the crown of the tree should be. An unnatural light. You could tell that this was the case because it formed a perfect circle.

To deny them would be to deny herself. She looked down but everything there was frozen in time. Balanced and motionless in the static branches, a smile of reassurance embroidered on their face. An intensity in their eyes, birthing stars. *Go up*, their expression read.

Go up and up and stretch for the light.

What else could she do? All that lay in wait for her below were memories.

She was no longer in the park. No longer in the branches. Reached up.

She crouched down in a lit tunnel. She could hear the soft thrum of machinery originating from inside the walls, which gave the impression the tunnel was breathing.

There was another light at the end of the tunnel, and it both leant the corridor a focal point and granted it some meaning. It was the shape of reality, the natural way of things regardless. It was everything her senses required, so she got to her feet and walked towards it. The light was a metallic teal when she really looked at it. She had an air of defiance on her face, or that was the intention.

"Is this a hack?"

'A benign hack

'My intentions are benign'

A shape appeared before her. Shimmering. The weight of the world pressed down on her. A hundred worlds.

She crouched down, hands scrambling on the floor for orientation. The shape filled out and increased in definition.

'Benign' the shape repeated, 'but my protocols dictate I require your permission'

"My permission…?"

'To begin'

She remembered their expression. On the tree. From the branches. Legs dangling, the world below refusing to be still, but somehow keeping their centre. And she surmised that permission was already forthcoming. Whatever this was, this thing of light, this *approachment*, it was in their head. This was enough for her. It had to be.

"Begin," she said. "Before I change my mind."

'The variant the random affliction if that is what it is constantly mutates

'Always one step in front I cannot isolate it long enough to break it down

'It assimilates it becomes the bloodstream it becomes part of them

'Humanity changes with it physiology adjusts in barely susceptible but profound ways and I take a snapshot

'I can tell you what it is not it is not a pathogen or a virus or a germ

'It has brought about something inside of humanity written into its DNA

'An expiry date'

This was nothing new. The bare bones is all. Perhaps the light was trying to assure her that they were on the same page. "I walk alongside humanity," she said, "but I'm not sure there is anything human about me…"

'Why a clone'

She found even though inside a virtual mindscape she had to inhale. Having taken one, she took a second breath.

"There is nothing to do. Humanity is dying. One hundred, two hundred years? No change in trajectory, it will be gone.

"We could augment them, make them into machines. But what's left of humanity will atrophy all the same, and what we're proposing is the cybernetic equivalent of papering over the cracks.

"I wanted to disrupt things. I wanted to see what would happen if we introduced a clone of myself.

"A normal clone can expect to live half the life of the original, so what does that add up to with someone like me? 150 million years? But my clone is no different from any human equivalent. What does this prove? That the planet is rejecting humanity in every form? The futility of the chromosome? Even my chromosomes?

"I can't change what is happening to humanity. I can't change the course. I, like absolutely everyone else on this planet, am faced with immutable truth.

The more we try to duplicate creation the less we understand of it."

There followed a period of silence. The shape before her would not be thinking, or something as crass as computing, but considering the options laid before it nonetheless.

'You have walked the planet since life first climbed on land you know as much as I do

'Something is different something has changed something fundamental

'But consider a point in the past in my relative infancy still a collection of minds tasked with making sense of the noise

'I searched beyond the mobile phones and GPS satellites and past the stars both alive and dead and FRBs and magnetars and bursts of gamma ray so typical of galaxy upon galaxy and I combed space for evidence of other radio signals from other civilisations and in the eventuality of detection I would catalogue such as *technosignatures*

'Observe'

A space map unfolded in front of them, forming hopscotch lines, that started at The Kármán line and reached as far as the Andromeda Galaxy.

'Located 2.5 million light years away from our current position is Planet 37 of Epsilon Andromeda

'Technologically advanced even from our vantage point of 2.5 million years ago

'A radio signal a translation designed for a civilisation to discover at a certain point not before

'It comes with the knowledge with a certain

advancement comes a certain degenerative state and the message says

'There is a place to go

'We have a cure.'

Her mind was reeling at this. The possibilities of it. The impossibilities.

"Even if…" she said, "even at light speed, to travel something like 2.5 million light years would take something like 2.5 million years. The journey will have barely begun, and what's left of humanity will have already turned to dust.

"Space dust. Earth dust. Dust to dust. What does it matter?"

The space map was presented to her as a series of scalene triangles. To stretch on to near infinity, or as far as her mind could comprehended.

'Please observe

'The secrets of the universe bound to simple trigonometry

'Encrypted within the signal is a method to bend light and separate space and time

'Where an object in terms of distance can occupy one point on the triangle and a different point in terms of time

'I believe it is theoretically possible for humans to travel such distances within their lifetime

'Like you Eve I am an advocate of disruption theory

'I am incapable of hyperbole

'Humanity is in crisis

'Rapidly approaching an endpoint on planet Earth where current levels of longevity unanticipated only decades ago have coincided with the switching off of receptors that enable reproduction

'An affliction'

"Wait." She scrunched up her nose. "What is this? A plot? Some AI-inspired conspiracy? To finally get us out of the way? To squirrel us all off-world?"

The onset of a non-existent heartbeat.

'We can debate conspiracy theories one eternal to another if you insist

'What we can agree on as certainty is if we do nothing humanity will fade and it will die

'I love humanity in every definition of the word as I know you do

'I was created by humanity but I cannot in turn restore humanity in any quintessential or meaningful way that it is not my purpose that is not my aim

'I want to help I want to avoid the inevitable for as long as I can I am eternity and I can do this

'Taking current projections the human population in twenty-five to thirty years will have reached an optimum level and after this society will slowly unravel and science will lose its prominence

'I have my window I have the technological blueprint I have what it takes to make this a reality

'I will reach out to the dignitaries and influencers and leaders and scientists of the world and share the knowledge I have accrued at the funeral

"At the funeral." She repeated the words, for fear that later she would convince herself that she'd imagined them.

'All I require is your permission'

"My permission. Apparently, this is what's important. It's as simple as that."

'Or perhaps we can debate the matter further we have time'

"Yes, we could debate," she said. She was no stranger to trying to restore calm, counsel kings, debunk conspiracy theories. Offering an olive branch. Sitting vigil at a bedside. A face on a TV screen. "We could."

A pinprick of white emerged from the centre of the shape. The otherwise nebulous light.

'Humanity has many things I do not have but I have to try

'It has one thing in particular'

"Which is?"

The white quickly expanded, swallowing the light whole and forming a perfect circle.

'Your gut'

In a world of technological marvels—of flying cars and clean energy; of self-administered augmentation and bubble droids; of plastic waste which consumes itself; of buildings maintained by an army of printers and living ink used in medical procedures—some things remained much the same as they'd always been.

Even as humanity came to terms with having an expiry date, and perhaps especially so, tradition still counted for something.

On the day of the funeral, they numbered in their hundreds; world dignitaries, influencers, leaders, scientists, all important in their own right.

They attended a large spherical building open to all faiths and denominations. The only request (not a requirement) was, if you had not already done so, you hadn't entirely ruled out at some point in the future making your peace with God.

Heads bowed as they entered as was the tradition, they took a nodule from the collection plates and placed it on their temples. This enabled them to remember Jane Gonçalves, the person, the hope, the ideal, in their own way.

The President addressed the congregation. "While I cannot claim to have known Jane Gonçalves well…"

Eve watched on. In truth, her clone lived a fairly ordinary life. What set them apart was providing a bridge between her and humanity. The people she walked among while living out the approximate of a life before hitting the reset button. A point of contact.

In the end, they would take Jane Gonçalves' ashes and scatter them to the earth. With the earth having little to offer in return.

They sat on mats, memory foam wrapped around them, supporting their spines, allowing their minds to detach from their bodies if this is what they wished. Sitting next to her showing his respects was Adam. He had travelled a quarter of the world, where he led a conservation effort to reintroduce the wildcat to the Scottish Highlands. He was a recluse these days from everyone except her. For an eternity, they'd both been on the cusp of history. Lining the layers. Traversing the rafters. Filling the cracks. Where else could he be at this moment but here?

One was Eve and one was Adam; at this point in time it didn't matter who was whom. They shared the same memories, feelings, actions. In another life, she was saving someone choking in a restaurant. In another life, he was washing someone's feet. And now their lives converged. She had finally caught up with him. He had finally caught up with her.

A foot or so apart, aware of the other on so many levels. Sparks of electricity sparked off one and earthed on the other. Rippling through them, causing their skin to pulsate. They grieved.

They were there for Jane Gonçalves, and they were there for the world they had called home for so very long, and perhaps even a tiny part of them was there for themselves.

"In our time, we've had to put up with a whole lot of shit," he said.

"Yeah," she said, "and I can't say anything will change.

"Hold on just for a little while longer."

They looked up.

*

"You go your way and I'll go mine," she whispered to herself.

If they had learned anything from their long lives it was that there were cycles of progression, restorations of equilibrium, the flourishes, the extinction events, the turn-up for the books. Always—that life finds a way.

They were as naked as the day they were born. Not nearly the same shape, and not caked in as much mud, but naked nevertheless. Naked and hairless.

She stood next to a tree with hanging fruit and watched as the Andromeda Crossing perforated the sky. The Crossing was a spacecraft the size of a city. A Russian Doll, layers within layers. Peel enough away and you would gaze upon its passengers floating in cryogenic suspension. Bodies preserved at minus 130°C, gathered up in bundles of light and dreaming sweet dreams of regeneration, representing the final part of the exodus of humanity.

Many ships, many cities, had launched on a monthly basis. The onset of time dilation would mean this last batch could arrive somewhere between five to ten years before or after any which preceded it.

From her vantage point, rooted to the ground, she blew the ship a kiss. There had been many kisses, many beginnings, markers of time, the circling of the ether. The cutting of umbilical cords.

She liked to think of them all as children of Khufu. She had lived many lives since, but none where she did not breathe in his dust. The more peaceful and quieter her surroundings, the more she was certain of this.

She placed her hand among the lower branches and found an apple there. Her fingers followed the contours of its skin, delighting in its smoothness. She wondered how sweet it would be to the taste.

How bitter? How vibrant? How red? But instead

she hesitated. She did not apply the necessary pressure. She did not pull.

Now that the world had emptied of humanity, the old world assimilated the new. The buildings and structures of mankind receded under the weight of it, becoming memorials to the passing of time and of departed civilisations.

Graveyards of decommissioned printers.

There were the advancing pine plantations. The boar, elk, deer, and wolves. There was a shift. A shift again. A resurgent ecosystem, the lush vegetation, the omnipresent undergrowth, unfurling like a flag of many colours. It passed through them. More green, and more teal blue.

And beyond, there was the ocean.

"It did it," he said.

She turned towards him but said nothing. She had a different type of hunger.

"AI got them off the ground. Every single one of them. Like it said it would."

He had to ruin it by talking.

She had to ruin it by listening.

"Do you think they'll make it?" he continued. "Will we take to the stars one day and check them out for ourselves? And what about us? Now there is only us. Again.

"I've worked it all out. It's not the fact we keep repeating mistakes, it's that we're still learning. We're a Work In Progress. Everything is."

She had the resolve now, to pull back and pluck the apple from the tree.

"Maybe we should start again? Do it right this time?"

She made to reply, body swaying slightly, jutting out her jaw in an exaggerated fashion, but she was only teasing. Tempting fate.

Instead, there was a crunch.

The apple tasted both sweet and sour. A little vibration originated from her throat. What to say, what to do.

"Race you."

She ran through the tall grass. She dreamed of the tide breaking around her feet.

AFTERWORD (TO EDEN)

The Concept album

I had this idea for a concept album. I'm the complete opposite of musically gifted, so the closest I could ever conceivably get to this is a collection of short stories all with the same theme. The theme is AI. Our relationship with AI. The backdrop is that humanity is slowly dying out, and AI is doing everything in its gift to extend the lifespan of the human race.

It's not as simple as that, though. I started writing these stories two years ago when AI was certainly a topic, just not the hot one it seems to be now. We have news reports coming in warning of this new existential threat from such as Geoffrey Hinton, one of the progenitors of what we now recognise as AI. Positioning themselves as children of Oppenheimer, what earth-shattering forces have they unleashed on an unsuspecting world?

And yet, and yet, and yet…

I'm as big a fan as anyone of Skynet coming to terrible apocalyptic life in the *Terminator* movies, but ultimately the psychotic bish-bash-bosh portrayal of AI in these movies doesn't make that much sense to me, either. AI is eternal, so what difference does it make to it if and when humanity dies out, or evolves, or whatever. Where's the rush? The immortality of AI is assured. The concept of time is very much a human preoccupation.

This was my starting point. This is what I had in mind when I started writing each of the stories that form this collection. As I got into the guts of it, I did come to realise that I had to be a little fast and loose with the premise, mix it up a bit. I didn't want the stories to say the same thing, so some of them do go off in other directions. I'm a sucker for a plot twist and where that may take me. But I think essentially, I've stayed true to the spirit of what I set out to achieve. It's just a little more evident in some and less in others.

And AI is never portrayed as perfect. Rather, the pursuit of perfection is such an imperfect thing.

This book is half the length of my second novel *the Light*, but took me twice the time to write. Too many prolonged breaks after finishing each story. Too much of lying in a darkened room, moaning, incoherent, the back of my hand wedged to my forehead.

The stories presented here are mostly in the order they were written. I've switched around a couple, but the collection starts with *Eden* and ends with *Rerun to Eden*, which was always the plan. The reluctant bleakness of the former and the guarded optimism of the latter.

Or is that the other way around?

The stories aren't linked as such, but if they do have a shared universe, they are each set worlds apart.

I have some notes on each story which I thought I might share. A little glimpse into the writer's mind, if not for your benefit, then certainly my own.

Oh, and what follows may contain the odd spoiler (like revealing the ending and whatnot), so I'm assuming as we're at the back of the book that you're reading this last? If not, why not?

Eden

An earlier version of *Eden* emerged as an eight-page comic strip published by Dark Horse in DHP#23 on April 2013. I was joined by the dream team of John Higgins, Sally Jane Hurst, and my long-time letterer, designer, and collaborator Jim Campbell. The version in this book goes into much more detail with regard to the characters and the world they live in. But essentially the core of the story remains the same—a man in a tower is joined by a courtesan while having to decide on the fate of millions. I remember one review of the comic describing it as the most depressing thing they'd ever read, which I suppose could be worn as something of a badge of honour.

It's a genre trope, one man living in a castle, a tower, a bungalow, but I've always been fascinated by the possibilities. In this case, our main character is detached from a dying world, but at the same time integral to the terrible decisions required to eke out its survival.

And while you're there, I should try and explain *the right side of pink*. The line comes from *The Great Gatsby* by F Scott Fitzgerald, which I've read several times, but not for some years. Now I think about it, the line might be *the wrong side of pink* alluding to Gatsby's questionable dress sense as he aspires to join the American upper classes, but even then, I wouldn't bet my comics collection on this (well at least that part that has the words *Booster* and *Gold* in it). Anyway, the point of all this is wanting to be true to the protagonist Aran. He remembers it like this because I kind of remember it like this, and I don't want to go back and check whether he is/I am right or not. A case of ignorance is bliss, but don't quote me on that.

Meat Space

The inspiration for *Meat Space* took root when listening to a podcast on BBC Sounds called *The Lazarus Heist*. This followed a group of North Korean hackers who spend the majority of their lives in cyberspace to the point this is home to them. The odd excursion to what we recognise as the real world is described as visiting meat space.

Taken in splendid isolation when writing the story, I would probably have gone for a more serious, grounded tone. However, because it comes directly after *Eden*, which puts the *see* in serious, I plumped instead for a more pulpy, grungy take on the story. I have to confess out of all the stories in this collection, this is the one I went back to and rewrote the most. Pinning it down was proving as slippery as an eel on a wet floor.

I only really settled on tone, I think, when I came up with *The Killing Joke*-styled ending. Where a giant arrow points down from the sky towards our protagonist with machine guns for arms.

You'll probably not even get the reference even if you have read Alan Moore's infamous/famous Batman/Joker graphic novel, but it's there if you look hard enough, honest.

Face of the City

The idea for *Face of the City* had been sloshing about in my head for decades, although I'll happily take a lie detector test and swear when I came up with the idea, I wasn't aware of the living, shifting, cannibalistic cityscapes of *Mortal Engines.**

This is a story about searching for identity—for both Charlie the protagonist and the city the antagonist. Also, like many of my and other generations, I am obsessed with the cult of beauty and I take this obsession and push it as far as I can.

There's something of Kate Bush's *Top of the City* to be found in the story's DNA as well. *Take me up to the top of the city, And put me up on the angel's shoulders*

*I can't speak for my subconscious though.

The Insignificance of Time Travel

Time travel is another country.

If you had a time machine at your disposal, would you choose to go back in time, or go forward? And upon going one way or the other, would you then decide to stay trapped in time?

Originally, I was going to write a time travel story where the main character goes back in time to kill Hitler as a baby, and on returning to the future, he is charged with infanticide. The main character is in a pickle as Hitler's war crimes are forgotten, or more accurately not recognised because they did not happen. As a result, he faces the death penalty. There follows a court case where the defence has to prove the unthinkable; that someone like Hitler and his crimes against humanity could ever happen.

In the end though, I didn't write it. I wrote what became *The Insignificance of Time Travel* instead. Once I got my head around the basic premise the story wrote itself. The idea of using time travel to relive the most basic of experiences again and again like that particular time you brushed your teeth, or emptied the dishwasher.

Eight seconds from human

I can't have a short story without a countdown, and here we are.

We're back to a grittier tone. A shittier tone, even, given the scatological nature at the start. Magnus is a despicable human being, who himself despises everything about him and the limitations of his human body. The only thing he doesn't seem to object to is the hunt, which he sees as his God-given right. Meanwhile, a bunch of politicians debate over the proposed elevation of a supposed sub-species to human status.

I suppose everything that I want to say about the

human condition and the wholly disproportionate influence we have on the environment around us, is in the story already. I left any notion of subtlety at the front door. Maybe it would be more useful at this point to list some of my favourite science fiction authors, all have had a massive influence on me. The list is endless, but the following come to mind: Jeff VanderMeer, Alan Moore, Iain M Banks, Ted Chiang, Jim Starlin, and John Wagner.

If I missed someone out, my apologies, just add your name here:

Manchester

A company I used to work for had their main office based in Manchester, and as a result, I visited the city many times. Because of the distance involved, I'd usually stay over. A few beers in the evening wouldn't be out of the question.

The city has given us precious things, The Smiths, Tony Wilson, *The Only One I Know*, but I have to confess, it took me a good few visits to warm to the place, but warm to it I did. In the story entitled *Manchester*, I tell the story of boy-meets-girl while the world comes to an end around them. This is my love letter to the city. You're welcome Manchester.

When Will I Be Famous

Okay, confession time. In *Manchester*, and unlike the stories which preceded it, the role of AI is pretty incidental. It's there, but plays a more passive role, amounting to little more than a cameo appearance. This was a conscious act on my part because I wanted to mix things up and...umm...keep things fresh...

And there was an element of such thinking behind *When Will I Be Famous*, although here AI plays a larger role, but really this story is just an excuse to wax lyrically and interminably on the trials and tribulations of being a writer. A world of social awkwardness, anxiety, self-obsession, and vindictive insecurities. When it comes down to the writer the usual, really.

Also, I'd like to think funny as in funny peculiar, and funny ha-ha. One lives in hope.

But fear not dear reader normal service is about to resume.

But before it does, one last thing, just to say the Twitter exchange in this story was actually played out on Twitter for real between myself and myself (I have two Twitter, or X, or whatever, accounts for my sins).

Two Weeks and Five Days

What would you do?

You've been granted a type of immortality, which comes about only by continuing to be part of a process. But your role is to bring the process to an end, and despite all the legal obstacles put in your way, you remain committed to doing so. But if such an outcome was to come to pass, you would lose your right to live forever.

Do your job and cease to exist, or take your foot off the gas and eke out a few more years...

I mean, what would *you* do really?

Rerun to Eden

Any self-respecting concept album will have an extended track at the end. Experimental. Ambitious. Epic. Possibly biting off more than it can chew.

For the title of this collection, I didn't want *Eden* or *Return to Eden*, because quite frankly there are about two million books out there already with these names. So, I thought *Rerun to Eden*, that has a nice ring to it.

It also set in place at the heart of it an Adam and Eve-styled story, but there at the end of humanity, rather than the beginning. It was always the case that the final story would end this way, even before I started the first one.

In the process of writing this story, I went down plenty of rabbit holes. There's always a level of anxiety (for reference see *When Will I Be Famous*) that follows you around as you write something. A little voice. *Is this working? Is this story coming together? Will anyone like this? Do I like this!? This is great. This is bloody awful.* Usually I'm thinking the latter mere microseconds after the former. The highs and lows.

The swings and roundabouts.

Rerun to Eden is easily the longest of the collection, and therefore generated the most angst. Originally, I intended to tie it in more with the stories that went before, but moved away from this the more I got into it. The more the two main characters took control.

The journey they undergo from the beginning (at least in terms of amphibians walking on the land) to

AFTERWORD (TO EDEN)   251

the middle (the last days of Constantinople) to the end (in the sense that the rest of humanity is in rocket ships and heading for Andromeda). And I dared to think, *Whatever I'm doing I think...*

Whatever I'm doing I think it's working.

Can you Adam and Eve it?

And with that last sentence, I'm acutely aware I've ruined everything. Okay I'm out of here.

But before I go, I would like to thank you for reading this little collection of stories of mine. Reading a book is a massive commitment and I am so very grateful to you. These are my stories and characters warts and all, and I'm incredibly proud of each and every one of them. I'm proud of me and I'm proud of you.

And now onto the next one.

Cheers,
Jim Alexander
Looking out at the Campsie Fells
2nd June 2023

Editor: Kirsten Murray
Proofreader: Elinor Winter
Production: Colin Maxwell
Cover by Colin Maxwell

Thanks to John Higgins, Stephen Slevin, Bob Heske, Ann Landmann, Will Pickering, Mike Richardson, Sally Jane Hurst, Jim Campbell, Andrew Dodd, Marc Olivent, Ian Bonar, Daniel Ings, Kirsten, Eli & Colin

Website: jimalexanderwriting.com
E-mail: planetjimbot@gmail.com
Twitter: twitter.com/JimPlanetjimbot
Facebook: facebook.com/groups/planetjimbot

The novels *GoodCopBadCop*, *Good Cop*, *the Light* & *Rerun to Eden* and graphic novels *Savant* & *Gabriel* by Jim Alexander are available from Amazon, Barnes and Noble, Waterstones, and lots of other places, including our online shop:
www.etsy.com/uk/shop/PlanetJimbot